FIND OUT
HOW THE PARTY BEGAN

You're Invited

DON'T MISS THESE OTHER GREAT
BOOKS BY THESE AUTHORS

BY JEN MALONE
At Your Service

BY GAIL NALL
Breaking the Ice

YOU'RE INVITED too

YOU'RE INVITED

too

BY JEN MALONE &
GAIL NALL

ALADDIN
NEW YORK LONDON TORONTO SYDNEY NEW DELHI

ALADDIN

An imprint of Simon & Schuster Children's Publishing Division

1230 Avenue of the Americas, New York, New York 10020

This Aladdin hardcover edition February 2016

Text copyright © 2016 by Jennifer Malone and Gail Nall

Jacket illustration copyright © 2016 by Marilena Perilli

Also available in an Aladdin M!X paperback edition.

All rights reserved, including the right of reproduction in whole or in part in any form.

ALADDIN is a trademark of Simon & Schuster, Inc., and related logo is a registered trademark of Simon & Schuster, Inc.

For information about special discounts for bulk purchases, please contact Simon & Schuster Special Sales at 1-866-506-1949 or business@simonandschuster.com.

For information about special discounts for bulk purchases, please contact Simon & Schuster Special Sales at 1-866-506-1949 or business@simonandschuster.com.

The Simon & Schuster Speakers Bureau can bring authors to your live event. For more information or to book an event contact the Simon & Schuster Speakers Bureau at 1-866-248-3049 or visit our website at www.simonspeakers.com.

Book design by Laura Lyn DiSiena

The text of this book was set in Bembo.

Manufactured in the United States of America 0116 FFG

10 9 8 7 6 5 4 3 2 1

Library of Congress Cataloging-in-Publication Data

Names: Malone, Jen, author. | Nall, Gail, author.

Title: You're invited too / by Jen Malone and Gail Nall.

Other titles: You are invited too

Description: New York : Aladdin M!X, [2016] | Summary: The girls of RSVP put together some of the best parties in town over the summer, and now the tween party-planners have been hired to plan a big-time wedding, but when a hurricane threatens Sandpiper Beach, all four best friends must gain a new perspective before this first walk down the aisle becomes their last.

Identifiers: LCCN 2015039805 | ISBN 9781481431996 (paperback) | ISBN 9781481432009 (hardcover) | ISBN 9781481432016 (ebook)

Subjects: | CYAC: Parties—Fiction. | Best friends—Fiction. | Weddings—Fiction. | Business enterprises—Fiction. | BISAC: JUVENILE FICTION / Social Issues / Friendship. | JUVENILE FICTION / Business, Careers, Occupations. | JUVENILE FICTION / Social Issues / Bullying.

Classification: LCC PZ7.M29642 You 2016 | DDC [Fic]—dc23

LC record available at http://lccn.loc.gov/2015039805

TO BROOKS O'BRIEN.
WELCOME TO THE WORLD, LITTLE GUY.
—J. M.

TO EVA,
THE EYE IN THE STORM
—G. N.

PLEASE SAVE THE DATE

Alexandra Elise Worthington
will wed
Isaac Jacob Malix
on Saturday, November 14
Sandpiper Beach, North Carolina
Invitation and details to follow

Sadie

TODAY'S TO-DO LIST:
- [ ] meet with bride
- [ ] back-to-school shopping with Bubby and the girls
- [ ] break Mom's heart

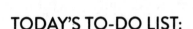o this thing just happened.

Well, not *just* just, but "just" as in yesterday. And ever since then I've been walking around with an iron anchor scraping the bottom of my belly that jumps every so often, because this thing that happened is either going to be the best thing ever . . . or the worst thing ever.

Or maybe even both.

It's also the reason I'm out of bed at six a.m. on the third-to-last day of summer. All the girls in our family—me, Mom, and my little sister, Izzy—are rise-and-shine, early-bird-gets-the-worm kind of people, but six o'clock during the summer is kind of a stretch for me. If Dad were still alive, he'd have seventeen pillows piled on top of his head right now, and nothing short of waving a can of coffee beans under his nose would wake him.

Mom doesn't hear me coming down the stairs, so I have a minute to study her. Her hands circle a mug of tea, and a few pieces of her hair fall out of a messy ponytail. She doesn't look like she's been up too long. She also doesn't look like she slept that well.

My stomach takes another dive, just like the pelicans circling the cove outside our window for fishy breakfasts. Am *I* the reason she was up all night? Not that she would know I was involved *yet* . . .

I tiptoe over to my bag and rifle through it for my phone. Mom still doesn't notice me.

Okay, so here's the thing. All last year I helped my mom with her wedding-planning business, and it was Awesome with a capital *A* because Mom is crazy busy and working with her meant we got to hang out together. I *thought* she needed me because I was her best helper. But then I made a teeny-tiny bridesmaid-overboard, seagull-pooping, photographer-puking mistake at this Little Mermaid–themed wedding she coordinated, and—poof—I got fired.

FIRED!

By my own mother.

But *then* my three best friends and I cooked up this plan where we would organize a party ourselves to get my mom to realize how totally fantastic I am at party throwing and hire me back. Except that didn't happen. The party happened—lots of parties actually, because after the first one went so well we just kept going with more and more—but Mom never made it to any of them, and she never got to see me in action at all.

Mostly it wasn't her fault, but still.

I flip through my texts, looking to see if there are any changes to our morning meeting spot. Despite my mood, I can't help smiling at a selfie my best friend Becca sent late last night. She's wearing a tiara. If I know Becca, she probably slept in the thing.

Because of Becca—and my other best friends, Lauren and Vi—it didn't even matter that much that Mom hadn't changed her mind about hiring me back, because our little party-planning company, RSVP, got so busy and I was having so much fun with my friends that I ended up having the Best Summer Ever and everything felt really okay. Better than okay.

And then yesterday happened.

I drop my phone back in my bag and turn, accidentally making the floorboard creak. Mom's head snaps up.

"Geez, Sades, you scared me half to death. What are you doing creeping around? More importantly, what are you doing *up*?"

I cross the room and duck my head into the refrigerator so she can't see my face. I don't usually—scratch that, I don't *ever*—lie to my mom.

"Oh, um, well . . . I'm just really excited for shopping today." Not technically a lie. Going into the city *is* exciting (okay, so it's just Wilmington, North Carolina, not, like, New York City, but when you live somewhere as small as Sandpiper Beach, anywhere that has dividing lines painted on the roads and four-way traffic lights passes for big-time).

"Oh, right," Mom says. "Back-to-school shopping. Hang on, let me grab my credit card. You remember the limit we talked about, right? Things are tight this month, okay? And Lauren's mom and Bubby will be there if the store gives you any hassle over using this."

She rummages in her purse and hands me the piece

of plastic. I swallow down my guilt as I take it. I feel extra bad going on a shopping spree just before she finds out I'm a total backstabber. I really need to get out of here.

I gulp down some orange juice and grab a banana for the road. "I'm going over to Becca's to help her sort her closet by color so she can spot any underrepresented shades before we hit the shops."

This is actually true. It's just that it's happening later this morning, not right this second.

"Okay, sweets. Have fun!"

I'm halfway out the door when Mom calls me back. Is she onto me?

"Hey, I just wanted to remind you: whatever you do, do *not* take Bubby's advice on skirt length. If it's not hitting midthigh when you sit, it doesn't come home with you! Got it?"

I nod and spin, making a run for the door and my bike.

My friends and I made plans to meet Alexandra Worthington at Salty Stewart's Café in the main square. Most of the businesses in Sandpiper Beach are clustered around the center, by the big statue of Merlin the Marlin, and down Main Street, which leads to the beach.

Merlin is this giant brass fish that's supposed to be a life-size representation of the biggest Atlantic marlin ever recorded, caught in 1942 by a descendant of our town's founder, Jebediah Bodington. If you live here, it's practically the law to know this stuff, but I get constant reminders every time I sneak behind the walking tours Becca has to give because her mom and dad run the Visitor's Center. Becca gets most of *her* information from Lauren, our resident smarty-pants.

I'm the first one to Stewie's (as we locals call it), so I grab the long table and wave to Lance Travis. He's going into seventh grade with us, and I have a sneaky feeling he's crushing on Vi, but she's way too blind to see it. His grandfather (Stewie himself) owns the place, his mom and dad run it, his older brother works as a waiter, and sometimes (like today) Lance buses tables.

"Water?" he calls over, as he wipes down a seat.

"Five, please," I answer.

Becca is next through the door, which makes sense since she lives closest.

"This humidity is inhumane. It took me for-*ev*-er to straighten this. I swear, I think the stars were still out when I started." Becca runs a hand through her red hair and grimaces.

Lauren and Vi push through the door one right after the other and grab chairs. "Who knew there was life on the island at oh-dark-thirty?" Vi asks.

Lauren looks at her funny. "Vi, this island had its start as a fishing village. In 1769, when Jebediah Bodington incorporated the town, it's likely that everyone was up at five a.m. trawling the Intracoastal for shrimp."

"Thanks for the history lesson, Lo." Vi sticks out her tongue and then ducks her head when she catches sight of Lance. "Who's ordering the liver?"

It's kind of a long-running joke among us, because Stewie's has liver and chicken fried steak on the breakfast menu, right next to pancakes and omelets. Don't get me wrong, chicken fried steak is pretty delicious for lunch or dinner, but for breakfast? Um, no. Except if you're Mayor Keach, who orders it every single morning. *With* the liver. Blech.

"French toast for me," I say. "But don't you think it would be more polite to wait for Alexandra Worthington?"

"Alexaaaaaaaandraaaaaa Worthingtonnnnnnn," Becca says, drawling out the name and using a slight British accent. "It sounds so fancy. What do you think she looks like? My bet is she's a total glamour-puss."

The door opens, and a woman teeters in on

seventeen-inch heels (approximately), wearing a hat like the ones you see on TV during the Kentucky Derby. It's purple straw and so wide it brushes the sides of the door. She's paired those with a tiny tube top that shows off a giant tattoo of some kind of bird covering her entire left shoulder and a pair of too-tight black capri pants. Whoa. I don't really know if "glamour-puss" is the right term. More like a weird cross between royalty and . . . I don't really know what. She's not a local, that much is painfully clear.

"Do you think that's her?" Vi whispers.

Becca cranes her head around. "Ooooooh yeah."

"Do we go over?" Lauren asks.

"I think it would look more professional if she comes to us, right? Just look busy. And important." Becca shoves a menu at each of us while throwing her head back and letting out a fake laugh that can only be described as "tinkling."

I peek over my menu to watch Alexandra Worthington's eyes sweep right over our table and then turn away to peer down at her watch with a frown. She's still hovering just inside the doorway.

"I don't think it's working, guys. I'm gonna go get her." I push my chair back and make my way to the front. "Excuse me, by any chance are you Alexandra Worthington?"

She looks at me and one eyebrow lifts. (I'm so in awe of people who can do that.) "I am. I'm sorry, I can't really chat, though. I'm supposed to be meeting someone, or rather, a group of someones. Though they're late, which is inexcusable, really." She begins to pick at a thread on her tube top.

"Oh no, actually, we're all here. See?" I gesture to our table, where Becca, Lauren, and Vi give little waves. Lauren's is a regular one, Vi's is more of a tomboy kind of hand flick, and Becca's cupped fingers and back-and-forth motion make her look like Miss America on a parade float. I can't help grinning at all three.

"Beg your pardon? I'm afraid there's been a misunderstanding. I'm meeting four women who run a wedding-planning business," Alexandra Worthington says.

"Party planning, really," I say. "You'll be our first wedding."

Oh yeah. The thing that happened yesterday? It's this: Becca, Lauren, Vi, and I were meeting at the *Purple People Eater*, which is what we call the old abandoned yacht that we turned into our clubhouse. The whole point of our meeting was to dissolve our little summer company and say good-bye to the Best Summer Ever. But then, right as we were toasting RSVP with glasses of lemonade, the phone rang and it was Alexandra Worthington, wanting to know if she could book us to plan her wedding.

Up till now, we've mostly done birthday parties for kids, plus a few parties at the senior center (where Lauren's sorta crazy grandmother Bubby lives), which were basically matchmaking ventures to get Bubby together with the elderly guy she was crushing on. They were great and we rocked them, but they weren't anything on the level of a wedding.

But when Alexandra Worthington called, she said she'd had been hearing our name all over town since she moved here in June. I guess people really liked the parties we planned, and, well, Sandpiper Beach is really tiny, and the rule of living somewhere really tiny is that you have to spend approximately 82 percent of your time gossiping about everyone else, so I guess word got out about RSVP.

Before the rest of us could even sign off on it, Becca grabbed the phone and said, "We're your girls, Miss Worthington."

Judging by how pale Alexandra Worthington just

got behind her tan, it kind of seems like the "girls" part might not have computed.

She takes a tiny step backward. Her head gives a shake back and forth. "No. No, no. No. No. You're . . ." There's a long pause before she says, "Children!"

Um, ouch? We're going into *seventh* grade. We're not *that* young!

Becca, Lauren, and Vi can tell something is wrong, and they all get up and race over.

"Excuse me, is everything okay?" Lauren asks.

"Everything is most certainly not okay," Alexandra Worthington says. I know I should probably call her Miss Worthington or Alexandra (though not to her face, of course!), but she's just such an "Alexandra Worthington" that I can't.

"I already fired my wedding planner." Alexandra Worthington is getting screechy now. "I can't go crawling back to her. I won't. That's not how I operate."

Oh yeah. If you're waiting for the other shoe to drop, here you go: The wedding planner Alexandra Worthington fired?

That would be Lorelei Pleffer . . . a.k.a. my mom.

So there's that.

Hence the iron anchor in my belly. Because when

Mom finds out her client fired her to hire her daughter, one of us is dead. Me because Mom has killed me, or Mom from a broken heart. Either way, things are not looking good for the Pleffer family.

Alexandra Worthington's voice screeches up another note. "Apparently, now I am *sans* planner because you are not at all what you represented yourselves to be! Why didn't you *tell* me you were a bunch of kids?"

Mayor Keach looks up from his liver, and Meg, who owns Polka Dot Books, turns in her chair. I kind of wish I could melt into the floor. Lance comes out from the kitchen with a crinkled forehead, carrying a tray of biscuits and sausage gravy. Becca, Lauren, and Vi share desperate looks.

I would be in on that look too, except at the moment I'm halfway hoping Alexandra Worthington will turn and walk out before this whole mess goes any further. On the one hand, I love my friends and I love RSVP and I'm still a tiny bit mad at my mom for firing me in the first place and then not making it to any of our parties this summer; if I wanted her attention, *hooo boy*, would this get it. But on the other hand . . . it's my mom we're talking about.

"Pardon me, Alexandra," Becca says. See what I

mean? Becca's never afraid of authority figures. She calls her Alexandra to her face. "But we never 'represented' we were adults. In fact, you referenced so many of our clients when you called to hire us, we assumed you knew everything there was to know about RSVP. Why wouldn't we have?"

"Well, none of *them* thought to mention you're barely out of diapers!"

Becca bites her lip and Lauren claws her fingers into Becca's arm to stop her from answering that comment with whatever she's about to say. Becca takes a deep breath, smiles oh-so-sweetly at Alexandra Worthington, and instead says, "Probably they didn't mention our age because how old we are is totes not relevant to how fantastic our party-planning skills are."

Which would have sounded a lot more impressive if Becca had skipped the "totes." Then again, if she had, she wouldn't be Becca.

Alexandra Worthington stares hard at Becca for a second, and Becca lifts her chin and stares right back. Neither one blinks. After a couple of seconds Alexandra Worthington's eyes narrow slightly, and she says, "You may have a point."

She takes off her hat, tucks it under her arm, and

pushes past us into the restaurant. "Where are we sitting? I'll need to tell you some things about myself if this is to be a successful client–planner relationship. First things first. I do not do liver and chicken fried steak for breakfast, and I sincerely hope none of you do either. If so, I will need to excuse myself because that is just plain disgusting and I won't hear of it."

Okayyyyyyyy, then. I guess we're hired.

Which is a good thing, right?

Right?

Lauren

optimism noun \ ˈäptəˌmizəm \
to be full of hope and confident about the future or
about something in particular
Use in a sentence:
I am full of optimism that this school year will be
the best ever!

*Z*ach's car wheezes and shudders as he hits the squealing brakes at the bottom of the circular drive that winds
in front of Sandpiper Beach Middle School, home of the
Pirate Pelicans. I grip the dashboard so I don't end up
kissing it instead. He inherited this pile of rust when our
oldest brother, Josh, went off to college. I secretly hope the
car will collapse before it's time for me to get stuck with it.

"A little closer, maybe?" I point to the doors, which
are way up the drive.

Zach slams the gas and then screeches to a stop in front of the doors. I still haven't figured out why Mom and Dad think that riding with Zach is even remotely safe. I'd be much better off riding the smelly school bus with Sadie and Becca, or cruising across the bridge to the mainland and down the main highway in one of my dad's golf carts from the marina. Somehow statistics on golf-cart crashes worry Mom more than statistics on crashes involving teenage-boy drivers.

"Out," Zach says.

"Thank you for the ride, brother dearest." I flash him a smile as I grab my backpack and heave the door open.

He rolls his eyes. Back-to-school might be the worst day of the year for him, but it's like Christmas to me. The tailpipe pushes out a cloud of smoke as Zach takes off toward the high school (which is all of right next door to the middle school, so he really can't complain about driving me), and I turn and head inside. By some miracle, Zach actually got me here half an hour early.

I stop just inside the doors and inhale that freshly-scrubbed-no-vomit-on-the-floors-or-anything-gross-yet school smell. And I feel like I could run up and down the halls cheering and laughing. Not only is it the first day of school, but all my extracurriculars start this week. I'm playing Bunco with my grandmother, Bubby, and her friends at Sandpiper Active Senior Living this afternoon, *and* RSVP just landed that amazing job with Miss Worthington.

Okay, so maybe she's a little on the scary side, but still—it's a *wedding*, and we're going to plan it. And maybe we barely have three months to do so, but hey, we wouldn't be the most amazing new party-planning company in the Cape Fear region if we couldn't pull off a simple wedding on short notice.

Besides, Sadie's mom already handled most of the major stuff, like the venue and the dress and the caterer, a long time ago. All that's left to do is pull all the small details together. Although that's really the most important job—they're the things that'll make the wedding extra memorable, and they're the most fun. The favors, the cake, the music. And I can't wait to get started breaking down the budget Miss Worthington gave us. Best of all? Vi, Becca, Sadie, and I get to plan this wedding together!

Life could not be any more perfect.

I salute the giant Pirate Pelican painted on the lobby

wall. (It's a pelican with an eye patch and a skull-and-crossbones hat and its wings are crooked like it's holding its nonexistent hands on its nonexistent hips. Seriously.) Then I find my new locker in the empty second-floor hallway. It's squeaky clean—probably thanks to Vi's dad, who's the new janitor this year—and full of possibility. I hang up the seashells I threaded with yarn last night, and stick a new dry-erase calendar on the inside door. Sadie probably has one exactly like it. Once I've gathered everything I need for my first three classes, I find my new homeroom—super-conveniently located just across the hall. It's totally a sign that this year is going to be the best ever. If I believed in signs, that is. Which I don't. Mostly.

No one's inside yet, not even the teacher. I grab a seat and pull out my phone. Technically, we can carry phones in school, but they're supposed to be kept off and in our bags. But no one really follows those rules. Plus, my day planner is on my phone, so I don't know how anyone expects me to keep track of homework and my life if I don't pull it out now and then.

Under the watchful poster eyes of Winston Churchill, Elizabeth Cady Stanton, and Ms. Purvis's other favorite historical figures, I click my phone on and check out my schedule for the rest of the week.

Monday, August 31
3:00 It's All Academic team organizational
    meeting
4:30 Bunco with Bubby and friends
7:00 Meet S, B, and V at PPE to talk wedding
8:00 Make Zach show me a computer game,
    but not one of those gross war ones
    (maybe while doing homework because
    how hard can a computer game be?)

Tuesday, September 1
3:00 Tutoring
5:00 SAT prep class
7:00 Create wedding budget
8:00 Watch TV (maybe while doing homework)

It all pretty much looks the same for the rest of the
week. I skip down to the weekend, hoping that maybe
things let up a little.

Friday, September 4
3:00 Founder's Day dance committee meeting
    with Becca at Chamber of Commerce
    (volunteer for ticket sales)

4:30–8:00 Work at marina
8:15 Have V, B, and S over for something fun

Saturday, September 5
10:00 RSVP meeting
12:00–5:00 Work at marina
7:00 Simmons family game night (ugh—try to
    do homework between rounds of Uno)

Okay. I can do all of this. No problem. I mastered balancing work and fun this summer. I'm a total pro.

"Did you really schedule 'watch TV'?" Vi's standing over my shoulder. Apparently, while I was memorizing my schedule, the room started to fill up.

"Of course."

"You're really going whole hog with this having-fun thing, aren't you? But doesn't writing it in your planner kind of defeat the point of loosening up?" Vi plops herself into the desk next to mine.

"It'll still be fun." Maybe she's right, though. Maybe I'm not having fun the right way. But if I don't write it down, I'll end up doing pre-algebra instead. Which is fun to me, actually, but my whole new motto after this summer is *Live it up!* (Bubby's words, not mine. At least she didn't say *Totes live it up, girlfriend!* or something else equally embarrassing for a grandmother to say.)

"Ooookay." Vi looks as if she doesn't believe me.

I slide my phone into my backpack. "Did your dad drive you?"

Vi sinks a little into her seat. "Yeah." The whole dad-as-school-janitor thing is still kind of a touchy subject with Vi.

"Hey." I poke her ribs with my finger. "At least now Linney'll have to use a solid navy fabric instead of orange traffic-cone stripes when she makes you a new moss dress." Linney is like Vi's evil archnemesis—if an archnemesis can come with a French manicure and perfectly highlighted hair. She asked us to plan her *Project Runway*–themed party this summer, but what she really wanted was a chance to embarrass Vi. She ended up making this awful orange-and-white-striped dress (a total jab at Vi's dad's construction job) covered in Spanish moss.

I missed the whole thing since I was home studying, but Vi told me that Linney had insisted she'd hurt her ankle and that Vi was the only one who could do the dress justice by modeling it down the runway. She pouted and whined until Sadie caved. Becca offered to do Vi's hair and makeup, and then Vi found herself wearing the moss dress in front of half the seventh grade. But it turned out that everyone thought she looked fabulous and Linney's whole plan more or less backfired. I'm sure she's been trying to think of a way to get back at Vi ever since. For some reason none of us have ever figured out, Linney thinks that not having tons of money is a good reason to make fun of someone.

When Vi doesn't say anything, I add, "Get it? Since your dad's new uniform is navy blue? That's so much better than orange-and-white stripes, right?"

Vi smiles, but doesn't really laugh. Instead she runs her fingers through her blond waves. "You don't think anyone will notice, do you?"

"What? Your hair or your skirt?" I ask. She's wearing a cute polka-dot skirt that the old Vi—the one who lived in running shorts, flip-flops, and a ponytail, and who'd have passed up a million dollars if it involved her wearing a dress—wouldn't have even looked twice at.

Her face flushes red. "*No.* My dad."

"Oh. No, I doubt it." Or I hope not, anyway. Logically, no one should care. Vi's dad needed a new job, and he got one at our school. No big deal. Except people aren't always logical. No one wants their parents working at their school. Having your mom teach science, like Emily Fenimore's mother, is bad enough, but having your dad be the janitor is a hundred times worse. Especially if your name is Vi Alberhasky and you've been putting up with Linney Marks making fun of you since fourth grade.

At 7:59, Becca pokes her head in the door and waves. She points at me, mouths, *You, me, dance committee!* and does a little hip wiggle before darting down the hallway to the homeroom she shares with Sadie.

At eight o'clock sharp, the alarm goes off on my phone. I scramble to turn it off before Ms. Purvis notices. Maybe I don't really need to set a reminder that says *School!* It's not like I'll forget to show up or something.

While Ms. Purvis goes through the usual back-to-school announcements and rules (don't run in the hallways, keep your phones in your bags, don't stick gum under the desks, don't put live animals in your lockers, don't dump sand in the gym showers), I look around the room to see who else is here. I spot Anna Wright, who's captain of the It's All Academic team. Behind her is Linney, who's twirling her shiny hair around a cake-topped pen from her mother's bakery while Ms. Purvis reminds us to get everything we need from our lockers before the bell rings. Of all the seventh-grade home-rooms (well, all three of them), Vi and I have to get stuck in the same one as Linney.

Homeroom is probably the most pointless period of the day. I mean, you don't actually learn anything. It's usually the class where I mentally walk through the rest of my day and make sure I haven't forgotten something important. The only thing useful about it today is get-ting books for all my classes. After paging through those, I go through all the vocab words I learned this summer to keep myself entertained. Finally the bell rings, and I can take off to English.

"What've you got next?" I ask Vi as we move toward the door.

"Spanish," she says. "Room 114."

"I'll walk with you. I've got English on the first floor." We squeeze through the door—where Lance is waiting for Vi.

"Um, hi," he says.

"Hi." Vi's looking everywhere but at Lance. And we're still standing in the middle of the doorway.

"It would be nice if some people could actually *moo-ove*," Linney whines from somewhere behind us.

At that I roll my eyes, grip Vi's arm in one hand

and Lance's in the other, and pull them both clear of the door.

"Finally," Linney mutters as she emerges from the classroom. She stops across the hall at a locker—right next to mine. Okay, this cannot possibly be a sign. If it is, I'm going to completely ignore it. Having to share the same general locker area with the most obnoxious girl in our class is *not* going to cancel out all the feelings of awesomeness this morning. This year is going to be perfect.

And it would be more perfect if Vi and Lance would actually talk to each other instead of staring at their shoes.

"So, Lance, where are you headed?" I ask brightly.

"Spanish," he says. "First floor." At least he's looking up now.

"Great. Same as Vi. Let's go."

Vi's face goes even redder. This is making me really glad that I don't have to *¡Hola!* and *¡Cómo está?* next period. Hopefully, in English no one will be making moony eyes at anyone else, and people will actually look at each other when they talk.

"So, um, are you going out for soccer?" Lance asks Vi.

"Hi there, my favorite Pirate Pelicans!" Sadie

arrives next to us before Vi can answer. "It's a new year! New pens, new calendars, new books. And new RSVP clients!"

"The books aren't really new," I remind her. In fact, my English book looks like it survived World War III, and I think someone actually chewed on my *Concepts of Pre-Algebra*. I almost handed them right back to Ms. Purvis and asked for less-used copies.

Sadie waves her hand, like last year's germs don't mean a thing. "Now please tell me one of you is in Mr. Grimes's English class next. Becca already ditched me for art."

"I am, and we were *supposed* to already be walking that way."

Vi and Lance are back to looking at their shoes. I really should just leave them here and let them mumble and stand in the hallway by themselves. They had no problem talking to each other before the Great Moss Dress Incident, so I don't know what's changed now. They used to joke around and speak in this whole other sports language that I never understood. But ever since Vi rocked that awful dress, it's like they've forgotten how to form sentences around each other. Becca swears it's because at that party Lance realized that Vi was cute. But

I don't see why that means they have to act all weird. I mean, if a guy liked me, I'd either tell him I felt the same way or I didn't. Easy, right?

"I'll go— Oh, hey, look! There's Mr. Alberhasky." Sadie's on her tiptoes, looking down the hall. She waves.

I turn, and sure enough, there's Vi's dad, in his navy-blue janitor's jumpsuit, pushing one of those bright yellow mop carts toward the lockers across from us. He's even got his usual Tar Heels cap on.

Vi actually looks up, and her eyes widen. "I, um, I . . . Let's get to class." She takes off without us.

"Hi, girls!" Mr. Alberhasky shouts as he pulls out the mop.

Vi stops dead in her tracks as pretty much everyone in the hall turns to see who's talking so loudly.

I'm so embarrassed for Vi, but I don't want to ignore Mr. Alberhasky, who's never been anything but nice to Sadie, Becca, and me. So I wave at him and smile. Then I push through to Vi, with Sadie and Lance on my tail.

I'm just about to ask Vi if she's okay when a fake laugh (seriously, it sounds like *heh-heh-heh*) drowns out the usual hallway noise.

"Is that *you*, Mr. Alberhasky? I didn't know you worked here. Sorry about the iced coffee." Linney stands right next to Vi's dad, empty coffee cup in hand. Which, I might add, we aren't even allowed to have in school. "You don't mind taking this, do you?" She tosses the empty cup into the black plastic garbage bag hanging from the front of Mr. Alberhasky's cart.

And he smiles at her. But it's not a real smile, because he knows Linney, and he knows how awful she's been to Vi.

Linney bounces—I swear, she's actually bouncing—toward us. "I didn't know your dad was working here," she says to Vi. "How . . . nice."

Vi gets this look on her face as if she's ready to pounce. I glance at Sadie, and without saying a word, she grabs one of Vi's arms while I snag the other.

"It *is* nice, Linney, because not only can Vi's dad bring her pizza and Coke for lunch, but she also doesn't have to ride the bus," Sadie tosses out.

Linney's laugh *heh-heh-heh*s after us, like she's some cartoon villain.

"I *knew* this would happen," Vi finally says as we round the corner toward the stairs.

"Please, you faced down her moss dress and her hideous idea of a cake topper this summer," Sadie says. At the very first birthday party we planned, Linney thought it would be hilarious to substitute a hobo and Little Orphan Annie for Scarlett and Rhett from *Gone with the Wind*. Vi was not pleased. After all, she was the one who'd ordered the cake from Linney at her mom's bakery, and it was pretty obvious that Linney had changed out the figurines on purpose to insult Vi and her dad.

"And you've got us to back you up," I add as I push open the door at the end of the hallway that leads to the stairs.

"And me, too," Lance says from behind us.

All three of us whip around. Vi's face turns all red again. I don't think any of us realized he'd followed.

"Your dad is the best," Lance goes on. He runs his fingers through his short brown hair. "I think it's pretty awesome that he's working here. He'll be able to come to all the soccer games."

And right then and there, I could kiss him. I mean, not really, because yuck. But he is one seriously nice guy, and I hope he and Vi can actually figure out how to talk again.

"Thanks," Vi mumbles.

"Well, if Linney doesn't lay off, I know exactly where to borrow another tube of green paint," Sadie says as we reach the first floor. She's the one who accidentally-on-purpose covered Linney in green paint during art class last winter when Linney made fun of Vi's green-tinged chlorinated pool hair.

Vi smiles, just a little.

We stop outside the Spanish room. Lance runs his hand through his hair for probably the ninetieth time.

"So, um, Vi . . . you know how Founder's Day is coming up?" he says.

Vi gets this wide-eyed, panicked look on her face. And she finds her voice. "Yup, it's the weekend after next. Okay, see y'all later. *Hasta la vista.*" And she disappears into the classroom.

Lance's shoulders sag. "Bye," he says all halfheartedly to me and Sadie.

"What was that all about?" I ask Sadie as we move to the next room.

Sadie grins. "I think Lance was trying to ask Vi to the Founder's Day dance. Hey, you want to go see if there are any new decorations at Party Me Hearties after school?"

I shake my head (and maybe shudder a little at the mention of Party Me Hearties, which wouldn't be so bad if it wasn't called Party Me Hearties). This is going to be one interesting year.

IT'S ALMOST FOUNDER'S DAY!

The most important day of the year for Sandpiper Beach!

Sandpiper Beach was founded in 1769 by Jebediah
Bodington, but you knew that, didn't you?

Join us as we celebrate our town's birthday with a
Founder's Day celebration for the ages!

Activities will include:
The annual early-morning King Mackerel Fishing
Tournament ◆ An epic town-wide yard sale ◆ The Sixth
Annual Sandpiper Beach Founder's Day Shuffleboard
Tournament sponsored by Shuffleboard Dan and
the American Shuffleboard Alliance at nine o'clock
sharp Saturday morning ◆ Afternoon sailboat races ◆
A delicious fish fry (all proceeds benefit the Sandpiper
Beach Volunteer Sea Turtle Association) ◆ All capped
off by the annual Founder's Day dance at the pavilion ◆
Post–Founder's Day Sunday brunch at the Church of
the Victorious and Forgiving Holy Redeemer

Festivities start at the marina at dawn and go into the night!

3

Becca

(Who needs a love horoscope when you've
sworn off boys!)

I watch kind of a decent amount of reality TV, I'm just
saying. And nowhere, in anyone else's version of reality,
does shuffleboard seem to be "a thing." Unless we're
talking *Adventures in Elderly Housing*, and so far no one's
made that show (although I might watch it if they did—
okay, I probably would, because I watch decent amounts
of *bad* reality TV). What? I'm just saying.

Anyway, shuffleboard is totes "a thing" here in Sandpiper Beach, and we owe that all to Shuffleboard Dan.
Way back in 1970-something (a.k.a. the Dark Ages),

Dan converted his entire front lawn into six shuffle-board courts (because five is never enough), and all summer long he sits in this little shed/shack/shanty thing he built next to them and dishes out advice to everyone he charges fifty cents to play.

Mostly his advice consists of "Be smooth when you push the puck! A light touch is all it takes!" or "For the love of sweet molasses, don't walk on the courts! You're ruining them! You're ruining them!"

I guess that last one isn't so much advice as admonition (sweet! I just used a total Lauren vocab word!) and Shuffleboard Dan's favorite thing to say. He probably yells it out in his sleep. If he had a parrot, that would completely *posi-tutely* be the first phrase it would learn.

But *he* doesn't have a parrot.

I do.

More specifically, I have Polly Want a Cracker, which is the stuffed beast molting feathers that goes along with the 100-percent-ruins-my-life-every-time-I-have-to-wear-it Dread Pirate Roberts costume my parents (who are *supposed* to love me) force me into when I give tours of the island for the Visitor's Center.

And which I'm wearing today because Shuffleboard Dan is paying me to, and also because I'm a teeny-tiny bit scared of him and his . . . er, enthusiasm. For shuffleboard.

I adjust the molting parrot on the shoulder of my puffy-sleeved shirt and *thwok* black pleather from my thighs. I swear, this costume is sticky even in February, but mid-September in North Carolina is—*blech*—the *worst* if you happen to be wearing pleather pirate pants.

I wave at a family approaching the shuffleboard courts. It's Founder's Day, and Shuffleboard Dan hired me to entertain the kids of any adults who wanted to play in the sixth annual Sandpiper Beach Founder's Day Shuffleboard Tournament Sponsored by Shuffleboard Dan and the American Shuffleboard Alliance. Try fitting *that* on a T-shirt. Also, I'm fairly certain there is no such thing as an American Shuffleboard Alliance, and Google agrees with me. I just know Shuffleboard Dan made it up so he could pretend other people share his obsession.

Anyway, obsessed he is, so employed I am. I'm not so sure the Dread Pirate costume was the best idea for this, though. The little girl I wave to looks fairly horrified. I'm pretty sure she's making that face at Polly Want a Cracker, but it's also possible that even a four-year-old has enough fashion sense to know the Dread Pirate costume should stay locked in a dark closet f-o-r-e-v-e-r.

I wave at her again, and she hides behind her mother's leg.

Le sigh.

I'd rather be wedding planning, even though we've been spending kind of all our free time doing it. At least you can plan seating arrangements and brainstorm ideas for centerpieces in a tank top. I head back to my beach chair next to the shed/shanty/shack and perch on the edge of the seat. Any farther back and the pleather sticks. Sooooo not a pretty sight when I have to get up. I wish Sadie would hurry up and get here; she promised moral support.

Usually I looooooove Founder's Day. The whole town comes out to celebrate Sandpiper Beach with a morning fishing competition, followed by a town-wide yard sale, followed by an afternoon sailboat race, followed by yet another fish fry (obligatory at every major and minor holiday around here), followed by a dance.

I got up early for the yard sale. Anything with the word "sale" in it—count me in! I mean, c'mon, it's shopping . . . on the cheap (even if some people drag the same stuff back out year after year and try to foist it on the rest of us!). But I live next door to a bookstore, and you should just see what they put out. The best.

This year I decided all interesting people have collections and therefore I need one ASAP. Lauren has a really cool shell one, so I can't steal that idea. Instead I bought three old-timey brooches from Mrs. Atwater (who called them costume jewelry) and a cloudy purple glass bottle that Mr. Vinton told me washed up on the shore with a message in it. He winked when he said it, though, so I don't believe him. But a beach-bottle collection could be cool. Or brooches. I haven't decided yet. A girl would do well to keep her options open (which is a saying of my mother's I'm totes adopting as my own).

Zero chance I was going to the fishing competition because . . . eww, fishing. Even though squishing hooks through worm guts and out of fishy mouths is totally horrendous, I *will* be hitting up the fish fry, because fried fish = super yummy and because Daddy gives the Founder's Day toast.

And of course I'll be at the dance, too. With my friends. NOT with a boy.

I've sworn off boys.

Which, omigosh, is sooooooo completely freeing. I have, like, 137 percent more brain space now that I'm not thinking about cute-boy things, such as the way they flip their hair when they come out of the ocean with their surfboards tucked under their arms. Who even wants to spend time thinking about *that*?

My entire existence is *worlds* better now that I've realized I don't need boys—or, more specifically, *a* boy—to write awesomesauce song lyrics about (song-writing is kind of my thing) because I can just write songs about different kinds of love. Like my mad love for my music, or for Sadie, Vi, and Lauren, or for shuffleboard.

Oh, no, wait. No one has mad love for shuffleboard. Except Shuffleboard Dan. And possibly Lance.

I spy him over by the sticks. (Sorry, Shuffleboard Dan. They might be called "tangs" officially, but that is sooo not catching on.) He's picking each one up and carefully inspecting it. Lance is totally convinced that this is the year he will beat Shuffleboard Dan. I should mention that Lance was also positive he would take down Shuffleboard Dan last year and the year before that and probably the year before that, too. If I were a betting girl (which I so totally would be if Daddy would let me), my money would be on Shuffleboard Dan.

Vi's money would be on Lance.

She glides up on her bike, all cool in her shorts and

bathing-suit top, with her hair twisted into a soggy bun that lets me know she got out of the ocean for this.

"Arrrrr," she says.

"Hardy-har. Talk Like a Pirate Day isn't for another week." (These are things you know when you live in Sandpiper Beach and most of your tourist money comes from all things pirate-y. We're always looking for stuff to turn into holidays, and TLAPD is another one. Ahoy, matey.)

"Well, if the pleather pants fit . . . ," Vi says, hiding a smile as she stares pointedly at my legs.

"If they fit, they would be even more uncomfortable. Baggy pleather is bad enough. But tight pleather?" I shudder. "Hey, did you see Lance?"

"Who? Oh, Lance is here?"

Vi is fooling exactly no one. We both know full well he is, and we also know full well it's the reason *she's* here. She turns to where Lance is weighing a puck in each hand and blushes six ways to Sunday when he catches her eye and gives a quick head nod.

Ah, young love. I'm so happy I don't have to worry about any of that. So, so, soooo happy. Happi*est*, really.

"Excusez-moi, pirate girl. Eez ziss where I can pay for zee shuffleboard game?"

I tip my head back in my chair to see who in Sand-piper Beach would be talking with a French accent and am suddenly staring into the warmest pair of espresso-bean/Labrador-puppy/brown-as-melted-hot-chocolate eyes I've ever seen. Attached to a boy. A my-age boy. And when my head tip turns into something more like a crane, I topple backward in my beach chair and end up with my Dread Pirate boots waving in the air at Mr. Oh-My-Gosh-He's-French.

"Are you . . . Can I help you?" he asks, as he crouches down and gently extracts Polly Want a Cracker's claws from my shoulder.

"Mmmmm-fffffff," I answer. What? Like anyone in my position would manage anything better. He's French and he's cute. There should be a law against that. You should be allowed to be one or the other. Not both. Sooooo not both.

Vi giggles and tugs me up. "Sorry about Becca. She must have hit her head when she fell." She elbows me, and I regain the ability to form a sentence.

"Arrrr."

Okay, well, maybe not a sentence, but at least a word. Sort of.

"I thought Talk Like a Pirate Day wasn't until next

week, Becs." Vi's still grinning like she thinks this is the funniest situation in the world. Like I am not standing in front of a French hottie while wearing a seventeen-sizes-too-big Dread Pirate costume and mumbling incoherent phrases. Words. Whatever.

I'll be killing her later.

"I'm Philippe," the cute boy says. Of course he is. *Of course* he has a perfect French name to match his perfect French accent. What *is* it with me and accents? They're like my kryptonite. First there was Ryan this summer, who was visiting from Ireland. Even now, when we Skype to work on songs together, his accent still does this weird flip-floppy thing to my stomach, although we are a thousand percent *just* good friends.

Philippe has his hands in his pockets, and he's rocking back and forth a tiny bit on the balls of his feet, with this confident little smile in the corners of his mouth. Daddy says boys with corner smiles are trouble. Well, Daddy says all boys are trouble. He doesn't really make distinctions. But still.

You know what? It's a totally good thing I've sworn off boys, then. Yup, totally, totally good thing. Plus, tourist boys = not worth my time. They just pack up and leave at the end of the summer. Although the end of the summer happened weeks ago, so France must have extra-weird vacation schedules. But whatever.

Once I remember the tourists-aren't-worth-it thing, I can totes be myself again. Phew!

"Hi, Philippe. I'm Becca. This is Vi. Are you entering the tournament?"

"Yes, I am. I thought eet would be a good way to meet zee ozzer kids in my new hometown."

New hometown? *New hometown??*

Um . . . say what now?

Vi

4

PIZZA ROLLS

The best thing about this recipe is that you don't
   have to measure anything!

Ingredients:

1 roll of crescent dough

olive oil (to brush on the dough)

pizza sauce

basil

oregano

mozzarella cheese (shredded)

your favorite pizza toppings: pepperoni,
   mushrooms, green pepper pieces, anything!

Preheat oven to 350 degrees. Unroll the crescent dough
and separate it into rectangles (two crescents per rectangle). Brush each rectangle with a little olive oil; then
sprinkle them with just a little basil and oregano. Spoon

a very thin layer of pizza sauce on each rectangle (not too much, or it will leak out as the rolls bake!). Then layer on the cheese and each of your favorite ingredients. Remember not to put too much on the rectangle, or you won't be able to roll it up. Roll each rectangle into a tight roll. Place rolls on a baking sheet and refrigerate for 25 minutes. Then cut each roll in half (make sure halves don't touch each other), and place in the oven for 10–20 minutes, or until dough turns golden brown.

*This is the BEST party snack or studying snack.

**If you use a meat like sausage, make sure to cook it all the way through before adding it to the pizza rolls, or it could make you sick. And something this yummy should never, ever make anyone sick!

I never in a million years thought that shuffleboard could be as intense as soccer or beach volleyball, but as Lance gets ready to push the weight in the last frame against Shuffleboard Dan, I've got my fists clenched, and my teeth are digging into my lower lip.

Dad calls shuffleboard an old-people-on-a-cruise-ship game, but, secretly, I think it was because he always had to work and never got to come to the Founder's

Day tournament before. This year he was totally into it, and even won his first game. The new guy (apparently), Philippe, took him out in the second round, but Dad stuck around and is totally cheering for Lance next to Lance's dad. As much as I wish Dad weren't the school janitor, I can admit it's nice that he's not at work all the time anymore.

"Are they done yet?" Becca tucks a damp strand of hair behind her ear. "I am abso-posi-lutely dying of heat exhaustion in this thing."

"You just want to change into something cuter for *Philllliiiiippppppppe*," Sadie drawls.

Becca huffs. "I do not. He's cute, but so what? I'm completely, totally, one hundred thirty-seven percent done with boys."

"Mmm-hmm," Sadie says.

"Shhh, y'all." I wave my hand without looking at them. If Lance actually wins this, it'll be the first time anyone has *ever* beat Shuffleboard Dan. Who knows how much money is in that pot? Dan never takes out his winnings, just keeps adding to it every year. There's probably enough to buy twenty surfboards.

Lance wipes his face with his shirt. It's completely silent at the game board. Shuffleboard Dan is a total stickler for the rules, which means the players can't talk to each other while the game is on. Lance exhales, and then pushes the weight. It slides across the board.

It hits the 10 mark at the very tip-top of the triangle. As Meemaw says, even a blind squirrel finds an acorn now and then. Although Lance isn't anything even close to squirrel-like, maybe he's found his luck today.

"Yes!" I shout, and punch the air.

But the weight doesn't stop. It slides just a bit farther—off the board. And Lance loses. So much for the blind squirrel.

"You okay, Vi? I didn't realize you were so into shuffleboard." Becca pokes me with Polly Want a Cracker, who leaves feathers all over my shoulder.

I'm not, really. Shuffleboard is So Not Vi. Although, since a lot of things that were So Not Vi—like clothes and sparkly purple phones—became Sometimes Vi this summer, then maybe shuffleboard can too.

And now Lance is looking this way. Maybe if I seem completely busy, he'll go talk to someone else. I used to like to talk to him—about volleyball strategy or soccer tryouts. We're even on the same soccer team this year, since this town is so tiny that there aren't enough play-ers to support separate boys' and girls' teams. But ever since I started curling my hair sometimes and wearing some of Becca's pink-tinted lip gloss, he's been weird. Like he can't figure out what to say to me. The first day of school, I think he tried to ask me to tonight's Founder's Day dance.

But he hasn't tried to ask me since then. I know, because we've had soccer practice and classes together. So I was either completely wrong about him wanting to ask me, or he hasn't worked up the nerve to try again. Either way, I've tried hard not to be alone with him, just in case. Not because I'm being mean. But because it's all just so . . . *weird*.

I grab Becca's and Sadie's arms with way too much enthusiasm. Sadie winces.

"So where's Lauren? Is she too cool for shuffleboard now?" I try to propel my friends toward the street to get away from Lance, just in case he tries to talk to me again, but Becca wiggles her arm out of my grasp.

"Ow, Vi. I kinda need my arm attached, you know?" Becca shakes out her pirate-coated limb. "Lo was here for exactly fifteen minutes. She said she only had four hours of 'fun' time scheduled for today, and wanted to save the rest of it for the dance tonight." Becca rolls her eyes at this, and I kind of agree with her. Only Lauren could plot out exactly how much time she's allowed to have fun. "Anyway, her alarm went off and she sprinted away to take over fairy-lights-and-streamers duty at the pavilion. The Chamber of Commerce people didn't go for the idea of her selling tickets and instead put her on the decorations committee, with *moi*. Speaking of which, I need to ditch the Dread Pirate ASAP so I can make sure she's not TPing the pavilion with streamers and—"

Becca's eyes widen at something over my shoulder, and her mouth twitches into this I-know-something-you-don't-know look. And now Sadie is rubbing her arm and grinning like a total loon.

Oh, no.

"Hey, Vi," Lance says.

"Um, hi." I turn around and stuff my hands into the itty-bitty pockets in my shorts. Except my phone is in one of them and my keys are in the other, so it's more like I've stuffed my fingertips into my pockets.

"Thanks for cheering for me," Lance says.

Becca giggles, and Sadie shushes her. And I just want to find a way out of here. "Sure. So, look, I gotta—"

"Wait," he says. "I need to ask you something." He draws up this huge breath like he's about to dive into the deep end of the pool.

Oh, no. Oh, no no no no. It's happening. I glance at Sadie for help. She grins at me before she grabs Becca's arm and tugs her away, leaving me completely and totally alone with Lance.

I glance at him, but he looks like he's in pain or something. So I stare at my flip-flops and pink-painted toenails.

"So . . . um . . ." He pauses, and I feel so warm that it's like someone just turned on the heat outside.

"Youwannagotothedancewithme?" He says it so fast I can barely understand him.

I look up, pretty sure my face is rivaling the red in Shuffleboard Dan's Hawaiian shirt. I open my mouth, but nothing comes out. Which is So Not Vi.

Sadie and Becca are standing off to the side, watching the whole thing. Polly bobs on Becca's shoulder as Becca bounces on her toes.

"Vi?" Lance asks.

I open my mouth again. No words.

So I do the next best thing. I turn around and sprint toward my bike. Then I take off down Pelican Street.

I hope he knows that means yes.

I should've said no. I should've said that I needed to practice drills for soccer, or figured out where to buy a guest book of least one hundred light pink pages with a cover embedded in Swarovski crystals for Miss Worthington's wedding (her actual request), or make baked spaghetti for five hundred people at the post–Founder's Day brunch at the Church of the Victorious and Forgiving Holy Redeemer tomorrow, or plot revenge against Linney for how awful she's been about my dad the first two weeks of school, or repaint my toenails. Or something. Anything. Because nothing could possibly be more awkward than standing here in a shiny silver-and-pink dress (lent from Becca) and shiny silver shoes (from Sadie) with my hair in a perfectly messy-chic ponytail (all me, but with comments from Becca), not talking to Lance, who is standing right next to me.

When I got home after the disaster at Shuffleboard Dan's this morning, I started to think that maybe Lance didn't know that I really wanted to go to the dance with him. So I texted Becca, who told me I needed to tell him right away or the world might end (meaning, he wouldn't know and would probably be mad at me forever—Becca kind of likes to exaggerate where boys are concerned). I skipped the fish fry and went for a quick run instead. Then I channeled my inner Becca, gathered up all the courage I had, and sent Lance a text before I could chicken out.

Sry I left so fast. Thought I left the oven on @ home. It was a lie, but it was going to help me save face, and maybe make him feel less like I ditched him. I pressed send, and before he could write back, I added, Yes 2 the dance.

My phone was silent for about half an hour, and I was pretty sure that meant he was really mad at me. But it dinged just as I'd started to mix up some pizza dough.

K. Meet u there. Another text followed almost right away. Maybe don't run away again? Guys on team heard & now they won't shut up abt it.

So even though running away sounds really, really good right now because this whole thing is super weird, I stay put. I wave at my friends as they dance across the pavilion to some oldies song, laughing and having a million times more fun than me. Lauren's bubby is right behind them, twirling around in Wanda (her electric scooter, which she named) with some of the other ladies from Sandpiper Active Senior Living. And then there's my dad, twisting and turning with Sadie's mom, who's actually smiling for the first time since we kinda sorta took her client—not that she knows that yet.

And even Linney looks like she's having actual fun. Which is saying something for Linney, since most of the time she looks like she's just eaten enough lemons she could make lemonade (as Meemaw would say). I squint at her in her short white dress as she dances by with Evan Miller, who's in this ridiculous purple suit. How does she do that? Actually act normal with a guy who's obviously into her? Because I just feel all weird and not normal right now.

Lance refills his cup with Coke for the tenth time and I clasp my hands behind my back so I don't twist them together. I have to say something.

"So . . . check out Evan's suit." Lame, Vi. Totally lame.

But Lance actually smiles. Then he burps. I can't help it—I start laughing.

Lance shades red, and I swallow my laugh. Now I've embarrassed him. Great. My friends whiz by on the dance floor again, and I wish Becca were here to whisper fizzy conversation into my ear that I could repeat to Lance.

"You know," he finally says, "I never got why this dance is at the pavilion. I mean, we're outside, right next to the dunes, and we're all in *these* clothes." He motions at his suit.

"Me too! It's weird to be right next to the beach in this fancy stuff. I feel like we should all be wearing swimsuits, you know?"

Lance nods, but I want to turn to sand myself and slip through the cracks in the pavilion's wooden floor. Swimsuits. I just mentioned *swimsuits* to Lance. Why did I do that? I might as well have said that I needed to go to the bathroom or something.

We go back to silence. I stare at the fairy lights ringing the pavilion. The town's conservation group lets the dance committee get away with the lights if they put up temporary walls between the pavilion and the dunes so that any late-season sea-turtle hatchlings aren't drawn to the pavilion instead of to the ocean. The pavilion actually looks really pretty. Maybe I should tell Lauren and Becca that.

Yup, they really need to know that. Right now.

"I'll be back in a second," I say to Lance. "Gotta check in with my friends." I don't even wait for him to say anything before I disappear into the dancing crowd.

"Vi! What are you doing here? Where's Lance?" Becca searches over my shoulder.

"I dunno. I just wanted to dance with my friends, okay?"

Lauren smiles. "Listen!"

It's Five Alive's "I'm a Hot Potato." Perfect. I jump and shimmy with my friends, and it feels like we're reliving our last party of the summer—the one where we threw a Five Alive boy-band bash for a bunch of eight-year-olds. Of course, our Five Alive was technically Lance, Becca's summer crush Ryan, and a couple of other guys from school, but they really worked it, and the girls ate it up. I dance and dance, and it feels nice to not be so worried about what to say or what to do with my hands or whether my hair is sticking up in back. It feels *normal*. Or as normal as it can get in a shiny, sparkly dress, anyway.

"How's it going, Mrs. Travis?" Sadie asks, a little out of breath as we dance.

I give her a good glare. "It's weird, that's how it's going. We don't have anything to talk about. We're just standing there. And my dad keeps looking over at us, which is even weirder."

"You never had problems talking to him before," Lauren says as she lifts her long dark hair off her neck.

"I know, but we always talked about sports. Or called each other names. I don't know what we're supposed to talk about when we're all dressed up like this."

"Oh, I don't know," Becca says. "Love. Fate. The stars aligning." She sighs, and Lauren gives her a look. "What? Just because I've sworn off boys doesn't mean I can't imagine being asked to a dance by one. And, Vi, since this is a dance, you should ask him!"

"Ask him what? About fate?" The whole thought makes me laugh. Like, *Lance, do you think our stars are aligned?* Actually, that would be such an awesome joke to play on him. And if this were Pre–Moss Dress, I'd totally do it. But not now. Because he might actually take it seriously.

"No, silly. Ask him to dance with you," Becca says.

"Oh. Um. No." No way. I'm not even a good dancer.

"You should," Lauren adds. "Because there's no reason girls can't ask guys to dance. And he's probably too scared to ask you."

"How in the world do you know that?" I ask her.

She shrugs as she hip-bumps Sadie. "It's something my mom told me about when she and my dad met. Which"—her eyes get this little sparkle—"was here, at the Founder's Day dance. It's like a sign, Vi. If those even exist, which they don't. But still, you should ask him now."

"I don't know . . ." My hair comes loose from its side ponytail and hangs in my face.

"Here." Becca reaches toward me to fix it. Of course, she's like barely five feet tall, and I'm closer to giraffe height, so I have to bend down. "Perfect. Now shoo." She waves a hand at me.

"Come on, let's dance some more. I only have three hours and fifteen minutes left before I have to go home and study," I can hear Lauren say as they dance off, leaving me stranded. I know they mean well, but this is just . . . awkward. I pat my hair and pull on my dress and pretend to adjust one of my contact lenses, and then I walk slower than a month of Sundays toward Lance.

He's still standing in the same place, drinking another cup of Coke and moving just a little to the Five Alive song. I kind of have to smile a bit, as I remember him dressed in that enormous basketball jersey with his hair all slicked back, dancing to "I'm a Hot Potato" at that birthday party.

I'm almost there when "I'm a Hot Potato" ends and one of those slow Harry Hart songs starts. And I slow right down with the music. Now if I ask him to dance, it'll have to be to *this*.

I turn around—and the girls are right behind me.

"Go!" Becca says.

"Destiny!" Lauren adds.

Sadie just grins and points at Lance.

He does look kind of cute in his suit, with his short hair all spiked up. And I can't believe I'm even noticing that, much less admitting it.

I can do this. It's just like asking if he wants to run soccer drills, or go surfing. It's no big deal, really.

I take one step forward, and Lance looks up and smiles at me.

I've totally got this.

And then a blur of white swoops in. Linney, all highlighted hair and enough meanness to scare off a pit bull, strolls right up to Lance, says something to him, and then pulls him toward the dance floor.

"Mr. Clean's daughter can excuse us for a minute, right?" she says as she brushes past.

Lance tries to catch my eye, but I turn away. My heart is sinking, sinking, sinking into my shiny shoes. I can't believe he'd want to dance with Linney.

I can't believe I let myself like him.

Sadie

TODAY'S TO-DO LIST:
- [ ] return Alexandra Worthington's call. Again.
- [ ] fold place cards
- [ ] practice calligraphy, especially *J* and *S*

*Y*ou smudged the *W*," Izzy announces.

Little sisters are such a pain. Even if she's right. I don't care that three of the last four presidents have been left-handed or that left-handed people are supposed to be more creative because we think with our right brains—sometimes it's just plain annoying being a lefty. Especially when trying to master the fine art of calligraphy in order to write out 122 place cards for the Wedding of the Century (so termed by

Alexandra Worthington at our last meeting).

"It would help if you weren't hovering behind me and breathing in my ear!" I snap at Izzy, and then immediately feel bad. I turn sideways in my chair and manage a small smile of apology. She flounces into a seat across from me at the big wooden table in our kitchen/living room. And doesn't smile back.

Sigh.

I've been trying to be better ever since Izzy told me how much she hated that RSVP was getting in the way of my big-sistering. Even if Mom did happen to pick us up after school a record four times last week, which basically hasn't happened in years, she's *usually* too busy to do stuff with us. Meaning we have to stick together, right? Except that's easier said than done with little sisters who don't even realize they're being bratty half the time.

Gah. Everyone's annoying me lately. Wedding planning is *hard*. This must be why Mom is stressed out all the time. Either that or it's my guilt eating away at me from the inside because I still haven't spilled the beans to her about stealing her client. Every time Alexandra Worthington calls to give me some new instruction (which is pretty much all the time lately) I have to hide my caller ID and run for another room.

She's totally suspicious, too. At Founder's Day, I overheard her asking Becca's mom if Becca had mentioned me talking about a boy. If only she knew!

My phone pings. "Oh for the love of peccadilloes! If this is—"

I snap my mouth shut before the words "Alexandra Worthington" can escape my lips. If I let things slip to Izzy, I might as well tape a flyer to Mom's forehead spewing every detail. Same difference.

"Who?" asks Izzy. She slides forward in her chair and props her elbows on the table as I glance at the screen on my phone.

"No one," I say, sweetly this time. "It's actually Vi."

And it is. Her text reads: rehash dance 1 more X w/me? Lo says she can't till 5:15, when her karaoke-singing time is over.

Poor Vi. She's still all worked up about how things went down on Founder's Day with Lance, no matter how many times me and Lauren and Becca pinkie swear with her that he was only dancing with Linney to be polite. What's way weirder is how unlike Vi it is to obsess over a boy like this.

I'm halfway through typing my Hey crazypants,

Lance clearly digs you and only you response when the phone actually rings. Not good. My friends all subscribe to the "text is best" motto, so the ring can only mean one thing.

I groan at the image of a screech monkey on my screen and slide to answer as I speed-walk upstairs, to get as far away from Izzy as I possibly can.

"Hello, Miss Worthington!" I muster all the fake enthusiasm I can. I may not make it past November's wedding date.

"Sadie-babe, I was thinking."

A large percentage of Alexandra Worthington's phone calls start out exactly like this. It never leads to anything good.

"Mmm-hmm," I murmur politely.

"You know how we were talking about a dessert bar with all different options, in addition to the wedding cake?"

"Sure. Yes."

"Well," says Alexandra Worthington, in her excited voice. Uh-oh. That's never a good voice. "I remembered these absolutely divine éclairs Ike and I had on our trip to Paris last year. He must have eaten six!"

I'm not that shocked. I've seen a picture of Ike, and

he definitely looks like he could pack away an éclair or six.

"I thought it would be a lovely surprise for him if we included those on the buffet. I already tracked down the particular patisserie in the fifth arrondissement, and they've agreed. Now, the only slight hiccup here is that they don't deliver, so I'd need one of you to pop over and grab them the day before the wedding. What do you think? Wouldn't they be divine?"

Slight hiccup? Pop over? "Um, I'm sorry. When you say 'pop over,' do you mean . . . um, to *Paris, France?*"

"Of course. And really, if whichever of you goes could take the red-eye back, that would be even better, because that way the éclairs could stay as fresh as possible, don't you think?"

"Oh, uh. I'm . . . I'm pretty sure none of us has a passport, but also, um, I don't think our parents would let us fly to Paris alone. But, uh, we have a new French kid in our class this year, and maybe I could ask him if he knows anything about éclairs that he could teach Vi. She can make *anything*. She's amazing."

I can't ever tell Becca I passed up an opportunity for her to get to Paris. It's practically her life's mission.

Alexandra Worthington is quiet for a second, and then she says brightly, "*C'est la vie!* Let's do that. Okay, now. Have I ever talked to you about peacocks? I love them. I was thinking maybe we could rent a few to wander the grounds during the reception. Peacocks are the ones with all the feathers, right?"

It takes me another five minutes to talk Alexandra Worthington into framing peacock feathers to display on the gift table instead, but I finally hit end on the call. Vi must think I've fallen into the cove outside my front door. I switch back to my text, but before I can type a thing, I hear a car door slam outside.

YIPES!

I tear down the stairs, forgetting I'm wearing fuzzy socks and throwing my arm over the banister to slow myself as I slip down the last three steps. I shout to Izzy, who's lounging on the couch with an American Girl catalog.

"Iz, can you help me put all this away before Mom gets up here?"

"Why do you have to put your art homework away? Wouldn't Mom be happy to see you doing school stuff?"

I puff my bangs out of my eyes and take a deep breath. "Can you just help me, please?"

A chime from the alarm on the door means someone just opened it. Noooooooooo. I take my arm and swipe it across the table, forcing all the place cards into a pocket I form out of the edge of the tablecloth. Izzy lowers her eyebrows and looks at me like I just grew a second head.

I make a *zip it* motion with my finger across my lips and place my most innocent expression on my face just as Mom thumps up the last of the steps from the garage and comes into the kitchen with two grocery bags. It's beyond great to see those, because that means I don't have to grocery shop this week, like I usually do whenever Mom is work-crazed. But it would have been way better to see Mom with grocery bags in, say, fifteen minutes. After I'd had a chance to clean up the place cards.

"Sades, grab these, would you? I think the milk is leaking and I'm afraid the bottom's about to fall out of this one!" She jerks her chin at the paper bag in her right arm and I stare helplessly for one heartbeat.

Then two.

Do I let go of the tablecloth and send all the place cards to the floor for Mom to see, or do I risk spilled milk and Mom wrath? What to do, what to do? Izzy is every bit as frozen as I am, looking back and forth between us.

Mom makes it easy by shrieking, "Girls! Don't just stand there!"

We both jump into action, but it's too late. The gallon of milk comes crashing through the soggy bag and explodes all over the wood floor and Mom's espadrilles. I jump back as it splatters my legs. Mom reaches across Izzy to dump the other bag on the counter, then yanks the whole roll of paper towels off the wall. She starts unspooling it and tearing big chunks of towels off to throw at us.

"Get up as much as you can, as fast as you can. Try not to let it get between the gaps in the floorboards. Moisture is really bad for wood floors!" Mom is practically frantic.

Izzy and I drop to our knees and start soaking up the milk with wads of paper towels. Mom joins in, and we work in silence for a minute or two until the worst of it is up. Izzy races down to the garage for the rags we use for washing the car, and together we get the last little bits up and polish the floor.

While Mom and Izzy are distracted, I stuff all the slightly soggy place cards under the refrigerator. To borrow Alexandra's expression: *C'est la vie.* I'll make more. Those were probably ruined anyway, and it'll be worth the extra work later if I can avoid detection now.

No one speaks until Izzy breaks the silence. "Well, you know what Dad used to say . . ."

"What's that, Izzy-fizz?" Mom asks. I smile. The worst of it is over if Mom's using nicknames.

"There's no use crying over spilled milk."

Mom rocks back from a crouching position onto her butt, and I wonder if bringing up Dad at a time like this was a good idea. You can never tell if it will make Mom laugh or cry. The edges of her eyes crinkle up, and I see a tiny tear escape. Uh-oh.

But then her shoulders shake, and I realize she's laughing. She clutches the leg of the table and starts whooping. Izzy and I exchange a glance and join in. The three of us grasp at our sides, we're laughing so hard.

This is *awesome.*

All the stress of the day whooshes away. Eventually, Mom takes a few deep breaths to collect herself and brings her hand down to the floor, where it brushes . . . a folded place card.

Uh-oh. I missed one.

She curls her fingers around it and brings it to her face. Then to arm's distance as she squints at it. Mom just started wearing reading glasses, and I'm betting she wishes she had them right now. As for me, what I wish for is an escape hatch in the floor.

I hold my breath.

"What's this?" Mom asks.

Izzy answers for me. "That's Sadie's art homework."

"You're learning to calligraph place cards in art class?"

"Um, well . . . ," I stammer. Mom's eyes narrow even more as she squints at the card.

"That's so weird. Isaac Malix is the name of a groom whose wedding I was planning before I . . . before I was . . ." Mom's voice trails off like she's trying to put her finger on something. She gazes off at a spot over my right shoulder.

I swallow the frog that has apparently taken up residence in my throat while I wait for things to click with Mom. She blinks and her eyes widen.

There it is.

Mom turns to me. "Sadie?"

It's like my brain has fuzz growing on it, and I can barely form a sentence that makes sense. "I, um, yeah. No. I mean, I was gonna . . . I was trying to . . ."

Izzy's head swings back and forth between us, and her forehead wrinkles like she's working a long-division problem in her head.

I try again, and this time all my words slur together: "It'sjustthatIwasgonnatellyoubutAlexandraWorthington-saidshewantedtoworkwiththebestwhichissillybecauseof-courseyou'rethebestbut—"

Mom holds her hand up. "Stop."

She pinches the top of her nose with her fingers and shakes her head. Then she takes a deep breath and looks at me. I can't believe this is all going down on the floor under the kitchen table, of all places.

"So, let me see if I have this straight. I was fired by my bride. Who then turned around and hired you and your friends? Am I getting it right so far?"

Mom's voice sounds totally even, so I can't get a read on what she's feeling. Is she mad? Or not?

I nod and avoid her eyes. Izzy inches out from under the table and slinks out of sight (although I'm guessing she goes somewhere she can listen in on every word).

"And when did this all happen?" Mom asks.

"Um, last month," I manage.

"I see." Again with that totally even, everyday voice. Like we're talking about what time high tide is or where we should order dinner. "And you didn't think it was maybe something you should mention to me?"

"Um..." I trail off and study my palm like the map to Atlantis is hiding between my life line and my love line.

Mom sighs deeply. "I have to tell you, Sadie, I'm very disappointed. Not so much about you planning the wedding, though I'll admit that I'm a little concerned about you taking on the responsibility of such an important event. I'm sure you girls are fantastic at what you do, but I can't really imagine what Alexandra was thinking. The part that *really* bothers me is that you hid it from me all this time. Did you think I wouldn't find out?"

"Well, no, but ..." I can't think of what else I want to say, so I close my mouth.

Mom sits quietly, waiting. After what feels like forever, she pushes up off the floor and stands. She folds and refolds one of the rags in her hands.

Finally she says, "Sadie, I've given you a lot of freedom and a lot of responsibility, because you've always been mature for your age. But I have to tell you, these are not the actions of a mature girl. You've broken my trust in you, and I'll be honest, it's going to take a while for you to earn that back."

The frog is back in my throat and it's settling in for a long stay. I can barely swallow. I curl my legs in under the table. Mom grabs her keys off the counter and calls out, "Izzy! Come on, sweets! We're going out to grab more milk."

I listen to the door click shut and the car's engine start, and, finally, it fades away down the street, but I can't move as tears slide down my face.

This is maybe the worst feeling ever.

First my mom fires me because I'm so incompetent. And now she full-on hates me.

SANDPIPER BEACH VOLUNTEER SEA TURTLE ASSOCIATION

We love sea turtles!

All residents and visitors to the island are invited to watch sea turtle hatchings! Please be respectful of the turtles and follow the tips listed below. Hatching times are unpredictable, so come prepared to wait!

Did you know that North Carolina's very own loggerhead sea turtles are an endangered species?

Tips for helping the loggerheads:

• Turn off all outdoor lights at night. The lights distract the baby turtles, leading them to homes rather than to the sea.

• Don't disturb turtle nests. Volunteers mark all known nests on the island, and the nests are protected by the City of Sandpiper Beach, Ordinance No. 17.2:1–4.

• Spread the word! Let others know about
the sea turtles and how to protect them.
• Alert the Sandpiper Beach Volunteer Sea Turtle
Association immediately (910-555-1772) if you see a
new nest or if an existing nest has been disturbed.

Fun Facts about the Loggerhead Sea Turtle!
• We can live up to 67 years old! That's over
four times longer than your pet dog or cat.
• Yum! Shellfish are our favorite food.
• We can grow up to 3½ feet long.
• One turtle can make an average of 4 nests
in a season. Each nest has between 100 and
126 eggs. That's a lot of turtle babies!
• Our two biggest fears: commercial fishing gear
and coastal development. But we're not
afraid of the dark—we love it!

*Come to the Sandpiper Beach Visitor's Center in the square
for more information about the Sea Turtle Volunteers.*

Lauren

dishearten verb \ dis'härtn \
to cause to lose confidence or determination
Use in a sentence:
I feel disheartened about everything I thought
I could do, even though I planned it all out so
carefully.

I am in what Mom would call A Mood. Since I turned twelve, she seems to expect me to be in A Mood all the time. She always asks me if I'm in A Mood when really I'm just reasonably annoyed or mad about something. Which I guess I am now, too, but the annoyed and mad feelings are stretching out way beyond the thing that caused them.

"Those baby turtles could outwalk you, Lo," Becca calls from up ahead. She and Vi and Sadie are already at the sea-turtle nest and setting up their chairs.

"I'm . . . coming . . . ," I growl. The beach chair bumps against my legs, and my water bottle is slipping out of my hands, and I keep dropping my jacket.

Fun. This is supposed to be fun. I am officially in my Fun Time right now. And it would be, if I wasn't in A Mood. But I can't stop worrying about whether I'm making the most of all my different slots of time. Especially the ones I've labeled "studying" and "homework."

I huff and puff the last few feet to the turtle nest. My friends are already sitting in a neat row next to some other people from town. The chairs line each side of the narrow length of sand the turtle volunteers have smoothed out to make it easier for the baby loggerheads to crawl to the ocean.

A little flutter of something happy tickles my insides. I haven't actually seen a single turtle hatching this year, mostly because I've been too busy with RSVP. When I was younger, Mom and Dad would let me, Zach, and Josh stay up late at least one night each year to watch a hatching. This is one of the last nests on the island that hasn't hatched yet, and word is that it will probably happen tonight. No matter what kind of mood I'm in, I'm not about to let this be the first year I don't see a turtle hatching.

"S'mores cookies, anyone?" Vi uncovers a container and passes it down the line. Becca takes three and hands the container to me.

"I'm not hungry." I pass it back to Becca.

She blinks at me. Sadie's head pops out around her.

"Are you sick?" Vi asks.

"She's been Lady Grumplepants all day long," Becca says. "She didn't even touch her milkshake at lunch, and you know we totes deserved milkshakes after running around all morning with Alexandra Worthington. And then she had nothing to say—nothing!—when Alexandra Worthington called about that Elvis thing."

After spending the whole morning visiting every place on the island and the mainland that could possibly sell or order wedding favors, our bride finally picked out bobblehead dolphins. Sadie ordered 120 from the store before Miss Worthington could change her mind. And then she had the nerve to call an hour later and ask if it was possible to move the whole wedding onto a boat so that an Elvis impersonator could parachute in, and whether that would break her budget. Of course it would break her budget, but I was too busy stewing in A Mood to say that.

Although none of us really said anything until Sadie

croaked out, "Well, maybe we could . . . ," and Becca said, "Elvis is pretty awesomesauce, Alexandra, but what if he landed smack-dab on someone's head or missed the landing and crashed into the ocean? And if you've got everyone on a boat, they might get seasick, and that could get kinda . . . messy. Plus, there are seagulls that could ruin everything."

And then, as Miss Worthington actually agreed(!) with Becca, Vi elbowed Sadie, who turned bright red because of the whole seagull-doo-doo/bridesmaid-and-dog-overboard complete disaster of a boat wedding that got her fired from Mrs. Pleffer's business in the first place. Though that whole thing is what led us to start RSVP, so who knows what brilliant idea an Elvis boat wedding could've caused.

Vi, Becca, and Sadie are still looking at me. Why did my not drinking a milkshake during my scheduled RSVP work time make them so suspicious? Suspicious: to have a distrust . . . oh, never mind. It doesn't matter anyway.

"So spill it," Vi says through a mouthful of cookie.

I turn away from my friends and toward the ocean. The sun's just set, and the sky is full of those beautiful dark blues and purples. Plus, there's a full moon casting a pretty trail of light across the water. Or it would be really pretty if I wasn't in A Mood.

"Lauren, if you don't say anything, I will," Sadie says.

I snuggle deeper into my sweatshirt as the wind picks up. Then I look around to make sure Mom and Dad aren't here. "Fine. You tell them," I say to Sadie.

Sadie takes a deep breath. "Lauren got a . . . bad grade."

Becca's mouth makes a little O, and I think Vi actually gasps.

"Don't worry, Lo." Becca reaches an arm around my shoulders. "You can make it up."

"I got a D on a test last year," Vi says. "We all get bad grades sometimes."

"Remember that C I got in PE?" Becca asks. "I mean, who gets a C in *gym class*?"

"Only people who don't even try to hit the ball," Sadie says with a grin. It's the first time I've seen her smile since the whole Alexandra Worthington thing happened with her mom last weekend.

"So what was it? Was it that pre-algebra test?" Vi asks.

I nod. The whole humiliating scene replays itself in my head for the millionth time. Sitting at my desk last period yesterday, trying to keep my eyes open because

Zach had showed me this crazy-fun video game where you can create people and build houses for them and get them a job and a family and have them cook turkey for dinner and pretty much invent their whole entire lives. Anyway, I got so into it on Thursday night that I stayed up way too late playing it—ignoring the alarm I'd set to remind myself to go to sleep.

After we spent forty-five minutes working problems on the whiteboard and then doing group work, Ms. Snyder started handing back our tests. Sadie got hers first. She held it up to show me the shiny A-minus on the front page. Ms. Snyder put my test upside down on my desk.

That's never a good sign.

I ducked my head down and lifted the corner of the paper to see the grade. And my stomach dropped.

Becca pokes me, and I stop reliving the whole horrible scene. For now, anyway. "Lauren, what was it? An F-minus? You know we'll still love you even if you flunk seventh grade."

Vi snickers and then turns it into a cough.

"It was . . ." I can't even say it. I look at Sadie.

"It was"—she pauses—"a B."

Becca giggles.

"Laur-*en!*" Vi says. "You got a B? *That's* why you're in such a bad mood?"

"It's probably the only B she's ever gotten," Becca says.

"It is. So what? Some of us have goals, you know. Like big, enormous goals." I pick up my chair and turn it so I'm facing the ocean, my back to Becca. My flashlight pokes me in the hip. I pull it from my pocket and flick it on, away from the turtle nest. Then off. Then on. Then off.

"Oh, come on, Lauren. It's okay. They're just teasing you," Sadie says.

"But it's a big deal!" I say over my shoulder. "It starts with a B, and then who knows what?"

"Then you end up getting arrested and tossed in jail," Becca says, her face all serious.

"Or you run away and live in a cave and forget how to speak," Vi adds.

"And then you have to, like, fill your own cavities because you eat too much coconut," Becca says.

"Yeah, and pull out your teeth, like in that old movie with Tom Hanks where he's stranded after his plane crashes!" Vi shudders.

"I don't think Lo can grow a beard like Tom Hanks." Becca shines her flashlight at my chin and pretty much blinds me. I twist back toward the water. "Nope, no can do on the beard front."

I bite my lip so that I don't laugh. I get it, I do. Getting a B isn't the end of the world. But what my friends don't understand is that now I'm afraid. Am I having too much fun? Are RSVP and that trip to the roller rink with Becca and video games with Zach and playing Words With Friends with Bubby ruining everything I've worked so hard for? Or maybe it's just that I haven't been using my study time as well as I should. That's got to be it. I just need to study harder, more efficiently. If I can do that, I can still do the fun stuff.

"Hey, look," Sadie says. "Is Lance hanging out with that Philippe guy?"

I move my chair back around to see what she's pointing at. Mostly I'm just happy that the attention is off me.

Both Becca and Vi shade red in the glow of their flashlights and look down. Vi toes the sand and Becca starts messing with her hair. Which is pointless since the wind off the ocean just keeps messing it up anyway.

"Ooookay," Sadie says. She looks over Becca's head toward me for help.

I shrug. It's kind of obvious that Becca likes Philippe,

even if she won't admit it, and Vi's been ignoring Lance for three weeks—since the whole dance-and-Linney fiasco. Fiasco: a completely humiliating failure—like Vi at the dance or me getting my test back yesterday.

We sit in silence for a few minutes while the turtle volunteers peer into the sand that covers the nest.

"We have movement!" one of them announces.

A ripple of excitement rolls through the crowd. I sit up a little straighter in my chair.

And then nothing happens for an hour.

As the beam from Bodington Lighthouse sweeps across us every thirty seconds, Becca goes on and on about Philippe's accent and his hair, and Vi keeps reminding her that she's sworn off boys. Sadie smiles as they talk, but it's not a real smile. I get up and move around Becca to kneel behind Sadie's chair.

"Hey." I poke her in the back. "You okay?"

She shrugs. "I guess. It's just weird at home."

"Is your mom talking to you?"

"Yeah . . . but it's not the same. It's all very 'How was school today, Sadie?' and 'Can you pick up some eggs on your way home today?'" She frowns. "It feels like there's something huge between us."

"Named Alexandra Worthington?" I scrunch up my

face so that I look like Miss Worthington when she gets one of her "brilliant" ideas. "Sadie-babe, I was thinking."

Sadie giggles—just for a second.

"I hate that things aren't right between you and your mom because of RSVP." I rebalance myself as my toes sink too deep into the sand.

"I could have said no to Alexandra Worthington," Sadie says. "And in a way I'm glad I didn't, but I wish it didn't hurt Mom so much."

I stand up and give her a hug.

"Sorry about your B, too," Sadie says, her voice muffled.

"Thanks."

"You're not going to quit, are you?"

"Quit? You mean, RSVP? No way! I just . . ." I smooth my hair as I ask my brain the same question I've been asking it since yesterday afternoon: Should I cross some of my fun stuff off my schedule? But I shouldn't have to, not if I'm studying harder. "I have to figure out how to make the most of my homework time, that's all."

"I know you will." Sadie squeezes my hand.

Becca grabs my arm the second I sit back down. Then she shoves her phone under my nose. The bright light is blinding, and I have to blink for a second in order to read.

Bubsters3000: My Lo Baby got a B on her pre-algebra test yesterday! Yayness! She's totes got the smarts!

"What?! What is this?" I squint at the screen and reread. It's not that my grandmother talks just like Becca—I'm used to that. And the fact that she can out-pop-culture me and that she likes to shop in the same mall stores my friends and I do. Used to all of that, too. (Mostly.)

"It's a tweet from Bubby. See, someone's happy you got a B—a B is good," Becca says.

"Noooooo . . ." I click the phone off and hand it back to Becca. Then I slump down into my seat. I can't believe Bubby would tell the whole entire world about my B. I called her yesterday to get some advice, but all I got was her being thrilled at my grade. I suppose that when you're used to grandkids like Zach and Josh, anything higher than a C-minus deserves balloons and cake and tweeting to everyone on the planet.

"She's proud of you," Becca says.

"*Everyone* is going to know now!" And I mean everyone. Our entire school follows Bubby on Twitter because of a party at Sandpiper Active Senior Living this summer.

What if one of my friends on It's All Academic mentions it to our faculty advisor? What if I lose my vice captain's seat? What if I keep getting Bs? What if . . . ?

"Flashlights and phones off, folks!" a turtle volunteer calls from the nest. That means something's happening. Baby turtles need to follow the light of the moon to get to the ocean, and they can get distracted by other kinds of lights.

We lean forward. I can just barely see some sand moving. After a few minutes, there's a rustle and an excited "Oh!" from closer to the nest.

"Look!" Sadie says.

I stand up with my friends and peer over Becca's shoulder. A tiny little sea turtle comes wobbling and sliding down the smooth path of sand toward the water. It is possibly the cutest thing ever. Once it gets to the tide line, it's bumped by the waves a few times before it disappears.

Sea turtles have it easy. Well, if you can get past the whole mother-turtle-laying-the-eggs-in-the-right-spot and not-dying-in-the-egg and then-finding-the-ocean parts. But at least they only have one goal: survive.

I wonder if I was better off when I had one goal. Maybe I have too many now, and that's what's wrong. The logical thing to do would be to pick the most important goal—excellent grades—and forget the rest.

But I don't think I can do that anymore. I'm not the same Lauren I was in June. I love RSVP and spending lots of time with my friends, and even just doing stuff that doesn't really have a point, like playing video games with Zach.

More baby turtles bump and slide down the sand. Becca practically squeals at each one she sees, Vi has a perma-smile glued to her face, and Sadie keeps trying to take pictures with no flash. There's no way I could miss something like this.

I just have to study better, that's all. Maybe even find more time for it. Time that doesn't take away from my friends or RSVP or anything else I love.

A FRIENDLY REMINDER!

Rebecca Elldridge's smile has a dental
appointment on October 14 at 3:15 p.m.

Terrific Teeth

Dr. Michael Bernstein

1215 Rosalinde Street

Sandpiper Beach, NC 28461

If unable to keep your appointment,
please give 24 hours' notice.

7

Becca

Daily Love Horoscope for Scorpio:
Sometimes it's only when you've given up on
your fate that your fate finds you.

Said No One Ever
lyrics by Becca Elldridge

That tarantula is the cutest
Said no one ever
This haggis tastes amazing
Said no one ever
I have too much money
Said no one ever

I love you
Said me never . . .

No. No, no, no. Nope. No.

I will not write a love song. I will not be the least, teensy-tiniest, microscopically bit inspired by the cute French boy who is currently invading approximately 94.2 percent of my brain space. Get out of my frontal lobe, Philippe! Shoo!

I toss my pen off the bed, where it hits a pile of dirty laundry and falls between a crumpled pair of skinny jeans and my yellow-and-gray-striped hoodie. I don't care who says redheads shouldn't wear yellow—I love that thing. Hey, I wonder if Philippe likes girls in yellow . . .

AHHHHHH. STOP IT, BRAIN!!!

"Rebecca! T-minus one minute until the bus! You're not missing it again today, young lady!" Daddy's yell has that *My coffee hasn't kicked in yet and I'm not in the mood this morning* tone to it, so I swing my legs onto the floor and hop between patches of visible carpet to my dressing table. I pick out my sparkliest silver clip to match my twinkling ballet flats and hook my backpack over my shoulder. At the door I pause, then double back for the yellow hoodie. (Of course I hold it up first to make sure it passes the wrinkle/smell test. Because eww.)

What? So I'm curious what the French think of yellow. Sue me.

As soon as Daddy drops me at school (um, yes, I missed the bus; I might possibly have been so focused on my hoodie that I forgot I hadn't printed out my English paper yet—whoops, sorry, Daddy), I hunt down Vi in the hallway.

"Did you get it?" I ask, leaning my hip into her locker door and accidentally slamming it shut. Vi gives me an exasperated look as she starts spinning her combo lock.

"Um, get what? Hey," she says, "before I forget, can you show me that thing with the eyelash curler again? I promise not to scream this time. Or I promise to try really hard not to scream."

Okay, so there was this day last winter when Vi discovered a nest of spiders under the front steps of the trailer she lived in before moving to her meemaw's. A whole entire nest of eight-legged creepy-crawlies. Did she screech? Call the police? Move to the other side of the state? Nope. She did not. She scooped the whole nest full of gazillions and zillions of creepy-crawly BABY

SPIDERS up in a newspaper and rode it to school on her bike handles so she could show it to our science teacher, Mrs. Fenimore. Now, I ask, how on earth could someone who has no issue with seventeen thousand twitching spider legs be freaked out by one small, innocent metal eyelash curler?

However.

Tomboy Vi caring about curled eyelashes is majorly exciting. She's like a tiny doe and I'm holding out my palm full of yummy deer food. (I have no actual idea what baby deer eat, so we're gonna go with generic deer food here.) But I know I have to stand extra perfectly still so I don't scare her away.

"Suuuuuuuure, Vi," I drawl gently. "Anytime you want. Maybe before your soccer game this Friday?"

"Before my . . . ? *Why* would I curl my lashes to play soccer, exactly?"

"Maybe since you're on the team with all those cute boys? And, well, since Lance is starting forward?" I hold my breath, since bringing up Lance around Vi these days is kind of a no-no. Her eyes burn lasers into the floor, so I change the subject super fast. "You never answered me before. Did you get it?"

Vi blinks and looks up. "Repeat: get *what*?" she asks.

"The invitation to my sleepover. I hand-delivered it to your meemaw's yesterday and left it on the back deck right outside the family-room door."

Vi's head tilts to the side. "Was that the purple satiny thing? What was that? I thought it had blown in off the beach."

I will not pout, I will not pout, I will not pout, I . . . "Off the beach?? It's a sleep mask. What would a sleep mask be doing on the beach?" I whine. Under my breath I mumble, "And it was lilac, not purple."

"Oh. Um, okay. I'm really sorry, Becs."

Vi does look sorry. Her eyes are all droopy. Hmm. Maybe I should catch a ride home with one of the high school kids at lunch so I can grab that eyelash curler sooner versus later. Happy eyelashes help droopy eyes sooo much!

I smile at Vi to show I'm over it. "Well, I hope you brought it inside, because I wrote the details for my sleepover birthday party in marker on the back. Get it? Sleep mask for a sleepover? Not that I'm ever, ever, *ever* gonna allow anyone to actually go to sleep, no matter how much Daddy begs us, but . . ."

Vi shakes her head. "Becs, we've been talking about your sleepover for weeks now. Even Lauren rescheduled her dance-alone-in-her-room time to fit in your party. We don't exactly need written invitations."

"We're party planners by profession now. We have a reputation to uphold. We can't skimp on our very own parties just because we're in the biz, as they say."

"They? Who's 'they'?" Vi tugs on the zipper of my hoodie as she grins at me.

I'm trying extra hard to think of a witty answer when someone shouts, "Oh, gross, Hunter!"

Hunter Crestling rushes past, clutching his stomach. About three steps past us he bends in half and pukes all over the tiled hallway floor. "Oh, gross" is right. It smells worse than the fish cannery on a July day. I'm so glad I'm not a sympathetic puker, because the smell alone is enough to make someone—

Fingers curl into my forearm.

I turn and peer into Vi's face. Uh-oh.

She's looking so green, no mere eyelash curler could save her looks right now. I forgot: Vi is *totally* a sympathetic puker, and by the way her lips are clenched, I'm guessing her stomach is rolling worse than the waves at the beach.

"Let's get you out of here," I order, grabbing her backpack from the floor and turning her away from Hunter.

She nods weakly and allows me to pull her down the hall, but she stiffens and stops when we hear a sing-song "Oh, Mr. Alllllber-haaaaasky! Your assistance is required in the seventh-grade corridor."

Linney Marks.

Vi's face was bad before; it's now a weird combination of green and blushing red that's making her skin look like an art project gone bad. When I try to tug her arm again, she resists.

"Can't. Leave. Now." She forces out the words between deep breaths of air through her mouth. Poor Vi. She's positively miserable. But I get what she's doing. She doesn't want to leave her dad alone in Linney's clutches. Even if it means he might be stuck cleaning up Vi's puke after he's done with Hunter's.

Half the seventh grade has gathered around the circle of vomit on the floor. The girls are squealing in disgust and the boys are pretending to push each other into it. It's only a matter of seconds before someone is going slip-sliding on Hunter's stomach juices.

Super-duper gross.

I hear Mr. Husky (Vi's dad and I are on a strict nickname basis) coming: his voice booms through the hallway. "Step aside, please." He rolls a mop and bucket up to the scene of the crime, but goes right past it and over to Hunter, who's still hunched against the wall. He puts his hand on Hunter's shoulder and whispers to him. Hunter nods and turns in the direction of the nurse's office. Mr. Husky grabs a bag from beside his bucket and sprinkles something on top of the vomit that smells suspiciously like kitty litter. Combined with the lingering puke smell, it means I might as well go home for the eyelash curler at lunch because it's not like I'll be eating anytime soon!

Once Vi's dad gets to work, most of the kids lose interest and start returning to their lockers. Not Linney, though.

Vi starts edging closer to her father as Linney's voice carries the whole length of the hallway.

"Wow, Mr. Alberhasky, it's like you've been doing this forever! Was Violet a sickly baby?"

And then . . .

"You know, Mr. Alberhasky, I was just thinking. My mom bought extra car fresheners last year when the sixth grade did that candle-company fund raiser. I'm just guessing that between all the stinky stuff your job entails plus Violet's soccer sweat, your car can't smell so great on your drive home in the afternoons. I'm sure my mom would be *happy* to donate some to you. I'll ask her tonight."

I curl my fingers into fists in my palm. Then I uncurl them just in case I have to hold Vi back. Mr. Husky gives Linney nothing more than a polite smile and gets back to the important business of kitty-littering boy puke off the floor.

Vi bites her lip. I know for a fact that her uncurled eyelashes did not have mascara on them before, but they kind of look like they do now from the way the tiny tears she's blinking back are making them glisten. I'm *thisclose* to finding something truly backstabby to say to Linney when I hear, "Linney, you should go by zee cafeteria on your way to class. Someone has put a cartoon bubble of you talking on zee pelican pirate, er, *comment dit-on*, er, 'logo'?"

"Mascot," Mr. Husky states, not taking his eyes off his cleanup.

Philippe nods. "Ah, *oui*. Same as French, zen. We say *mascotte*."

Mr. Husky understands French? More importantly, Linney speaks Pirate Pelican? Her mouth opens and closes like the king mackerel I *didn't* fish for on Founder's Day, and her mini heels click-clack on the tiles as she races in the direction of the cafeteria.

"Is that true?" I ask Philippe.

He shrugs. "Not unless someone added eet in zee last five minutes since I was there. But eet got her to leave, *n'est-ce pas?*"

Oh. My. God.

Philippe is adorable-looking, AND has an accent, AND is nice. Not just nice. Heroic. My hero.

Well, not mine, since technically it was Vi he helped out there, but . . . ahhhhhhhhh. Dumb boys. Why do they have to be so sweet? And cute? And accented?

I will not like Philippe. *I will not* like Philippe. I WILL NOT like Philippe.

He smiles and winks at me, then salutes Vi as he brushes past us. Then he looks over his shoulder and catches my eye before saying, "By zee way, nice yellow jacket."

Drat. I think I like Philippe.

Okay, so I *do* like Philippe.

No big whoop. I mean, it's not like that means he likes me back or that anything has to happen from here. I can just admire him from afar and go about my merry way. Yup. Yuppers. That's totally my plan.

Because I have sworn off guys in a grand effort to "get to know myself." It's only when we know ourselves inside and out that the truest song lyrics can flow. I'm pretty sure that's rule number three in the Taylor Swift handbook.

I'm repeating this mantra over and over in my head when my mama rolls up in her (bo-*ring*) sedan to pick me up early from school. Don't get me wrong, I looooooove early dismissals, but leaving school for a dentist appointment hardly counts. It's like trading bad for worse. Well, maybe not worse, because I'm a flosser, plus I believe in all the other principles of good oral hygiene, since white teeth are a girl's built-in beauty asset, which means dentist visits are pretty painless. But it's nothing like leaving early for a shopping trip or to head out of town. Terrific Teeth is just over the bridge from school, back on the island. No luggage required.

When we get there I settle back in the reclining chair and open wide so Jill, my hygienist, can do her thing with the tooth-scrapey doowat.

"Everything looks great, Becca," she says. "Keep up the flossing. I'm just gonna send Dr. Bernstein in for his check. Hang tight."

Dr. Bernstein installed these cool pictures in place

of the clear covers on the fluorescent lights on the ceiling, and the one over me is of a hot-air balloon taking off. I'm busy imagining myself with Philippe in the basket of it when the dentist comes into the exam room.

"Rebecca. Long time no see. Last time I spotted you in town, you were rocking an oversize pirate costume. You should tell your dad your doctor said pleather is bad for the skin."

"No offense, Dr. Bernstein, but you're a *tooth* doctor." He's so cheesy, but I like him anyway.

"Worth a try, Becca. Worth a try. Okay, now let's take a peek in here. Open wide."

He pokes and prods for a few seconds and there's kind of a ridiculous lot of *hmmm*-ing going on. What does *hmmm*-ing mean? When he finishes, he says, "Great job, Becca. Let's call your mother in, shall we?"

Say what now? This is the point in the appointment when I'm supposed to get a new toothbrush and a construction-paper cutout of a tooth that I get to write my name on and stick on the "No Cavities Wall of Fame." If Jill's in a good mood, she'll even forget the ten-and-under rule on the prize bucket and let me pick out a My Pretty Pony sticker I can (ironically, of course) slap on my binder. Every one of those activities is "no parents required."

My mother appears in the doorway, and Dr. Bernstein grins at her. "We knew this day was coming."

Mama grins back and makes a show of reaching in her purse. "Should I just hand over my entire wallet now?"

What exactly is going on here?

"What exactly is going on here?" I ask. Both turn to me like they forgot I was even present and accounted for.

Dr. Bernstein exchanges a look with Mama, and she nods. He takes a breath. "Now, I know this isn't the news every lovely young girl likes to hear, but, Becca? I'm afraid you're going to need braces."

Here's all I have to say: It is really a *most* excellent thing I'm already reclined. In fact, I believe I might as well stay this way and they can just build the coffin around me.

Because my life?

Is O-V-E-R.

Oh, Philippe! We could have been something!

SWEET DREAMS!

Becca's turning THIRTEEN and you're invited
to witness the occasion at an EPIC SLEEPOVER!

Where: Becca's House
When: Saturday, October 24, 5:00 p.m.

Junk food mandatory.
Pack a pillow, but don't think you'll be
resting your head on it!

Vi

8

CARAMEL APPLES

Ingredients:

6 apples

6 wooden craft sticks

1 14-oz bag of caramel candies

2 tbsp milk

1 small bag of chopped peanuts or colored sprinkles

Wash and dry the apples. Remove their stems and carefully insert a craft stick into the top of each apple. Coat a baking sheet with butter. Unwrap all the caramels and place them into a microwave-safe bowl with the milk. Microwave for one minute; then stir; then microwave for one more minute. Allow the caramel mixture to cool for a short while, and then roll each apple in the mixture. Once the apple is coated with caramel, dip it into the chopped peanuts or sprinkles.

Place the apple on the baking sheet until the caramel coating cools completely.
**This is a really great snack to make with little kids.*
**Or with friends who are getting braces and won't be able to have these for a while!*

linding sun streams through the kitchen windows as I pull the breakfast scramble from the oven. As much as I never minded living with just Dad in our trailer at Sandpiper Pines Mobile Home Park, I will seriously miss this amazing kitchen and the view of the beach when Meemaw comes back home. She was only supposed to be in Maine for the summer, but she said she was having so much fun with the friends she was visiting that she decided to keep the cottage she was renting up there for a few more months. When Dad heard, he frowned. He thinks she's only staying there so that we can keep living in her house. And there's nothing Dad hates more than charity.

While the casserole dish cools on the counter, I drop the exact number of scoops of ground beans into the coffeemaker's basket and press the start button. Sure enough, as soon as the coffee finishes gurgling into the pot, Dad appears in the doorway.

"Vi?" he asks as he rubs his eyes with the heel of his hand. He's thrown on an old Tar Heels T-shirt and jeans, and his hair is sticking up every which way. He looks So Very Dad that I almost chicken out on my plan.

Almost. All it takes is Linney's sneering face popping into my head to remind me that I *have* to do this. That girl really dills my pickle, and I can't deal with her making fun of my dad the rest of the year.

"Good morning, Dad!" I say, way too chirpily. "There's coffee and breakfast scramble." I cut a piece from the casserole dish. "It's got eggs and sausage and tomatoes." I drop the plate on the table and go to fill his mug.

He eyes the plate. "I see that. And it looks great, sweetie. But . . . it's seven a.m. on a Saturday. Why are you up?"

I carefully place the coffee on the table and then fetch a fork and knife. "Oh, um . . . I have soccer practice this morning."

"At ten, right?"

"Yeah . . ." *Come on, Vi. Just say it.* I've only been psyching myself up for this all week, and I have what

I'm going to say all planned out. I just have to do it. Fish or cut bait, Meemaw would tell me.

Dad digs into his food, and I fill a plate for myself. Except I'm not really hungry. I sit down and fold my napkin into triangles.

"This is really good," Dad says through a mouthful of eggs. He looks up at me, and I open my mouth to say what I planned . . . and shovel a forkful of food into it instead.

"Thanks." I barely get the words out past the food.

Dad's done in about three bites. He picks up his coffee and leans back in his chair. He's studying me like he's never seen me before. Which is so not helping. I push a piece of sausage across my plate.

"Oh wait," he says softly. "I know what this is about."

"You do?" I look up, really hoping he brings up the subject himself. That would make this *so* much easier.

He goes red under what's left of his summer tan. "It's about that Travis boy, isn't it? The one you went to the Founder's Day dance with."

I choke on the orange juice I just tried to swallow. Dad passes me another napkin as I cough.

"Now, Vi, sweetie, he's a great kid, and his family is good people, but you're twelve. And maybe I'm a little old-fashioned, but that's just too young for dating. I know it's weird to talk to me about this, but since your mother isn't here . . . well, I'm glad you brought it up anyway."

Except I didn't bring it up. I take a huge gulp of orange juice, partly to stop coughing and partly so I don't have to say anything just yet. Because Lance is not—not *at all*—what I wanted to talk to Dad about. In fact, he's probably the last thing I'd ever want to talk to Dad about.

I drain my glass. Dad's looking at me all expectantly, like he's not sure if I'm going to fight him on the no-boyfriends thing. Which is so embarrassing and so not at all on my mind right now. Mostly.

Deep breath, Vi. Just say it.

"Um . . . it's not about Lance . . . ," I finally say. And I swear Dad sags a little bit in his chair, like he's just dropped a bag of rocks. "It's about . . . I want you to quit your job."

There. Said it.

And watching Dad frown, I feel like the biggest jerk ever.

He takes a sip of coffee. I flatten out my napkin on my knee and start folding triangles all over again.

"First," he finally says, "if I did that, I'd have to go back to construction, and that means I'd miss all of your soccer games."

Right. I'd hate that, but it'd be worth it to get Linney off my back at school.

"Second, you realize that was the first Founder's Day I've been to in years? And I liked it, even the old-people-on-a-cruise-ship game. If I didn't have this new job, I would've missed seeing you get all dressed up."

That's true. Before we were old enough to go around town by ourselves, I usually tagged along to Founder's Day stuff with Sadie's family. It was nice to see Dad out that day, for a change.

"And third, didn't you buy us those kayaks so we could paddle together? I can't do that if I work all the time. And I like this job. Sure, it ain't a job that comes with an office or anything, but I like it. I like being around the kids and knowing that I'll get off work at five o'clock every day."

The whole time he's been talking, I've felt as if I swallowed a piece of gum. And that gum's been sitting in my stomach like a water balloon that keeps growing and growing and growing.

I'm starting to wish I hadn't said anything at all.

Dad drains his coffee and goes to refill the mug. I clear the table, as quietly as possible, kind of hoping he won't say anything else.

"I know I embarrass you," he says.

I drop the dishes into the sink a little too hard, and one of Meemaw's pretty shell-patterned plates cracks right across the middle.

"Dad . . . ," I start, but, really, I don't know what to say right now. *I'm sorry I don't care that this job makes you happy? I'm sorry I'm a shallow meanie who only cares about what people think of me?*

"Being twelve is hard," he says. "I get that. But the Vi I know—the one who plays a mean game of soccer, the one who's stood up to that Linney girl for years—that Vi wouldn't care." He holds up the lid to the kitchen trash can as I dump the two pieces of plate into it.

I want to agree with him and say that of course I don't care what Linney thinks. But then I flash back to that whole scene in the school hallway, with Becca by my side and that new French guy coming to my rescue.

Maybe that's it. Maybe I don't want to be rescued. But it wasn't as if I was standing up for myself right then. And I don't know why I wasn't.

"So I'm sorry if my job embarrasses you, but I'm not

going to quit." Dad puts his mug into the sink. "Thank
you for breakfast."

And then he's gone.

If it hadn't been crack-of-dawn a.m. and if I didn't have
practice in a few hours, I would've sent the Bat Signal
to Sadie, Lauren, and Becca. Instead I baked six dozen
muffins for no reason, and then Dad drove me to soccer. After the most uncomfortable car ride ever, I had
to spend the whole practice ignoring Lance, who kept
staring at me every time we got anywhere near each
other. I don't even know why—it's not as if he likes me.
He made it pretty clear at the Founder's Day dance that
he's into Linney. And ever since then, she's been eating lunch at his table. Mostly, I pretend to ignore them,
because it's easier that way.

I snagged a ride home with Evan Miller, so at least
I didn't have to feel so guilty sitting next to Dad again.
His new green kayak was gone when I got back, too.
So I texted Lauren, who talked to me for a few minutes
before her alarm went off to remind her that it was time
to finish her pre-algebra homework. Then I got ready
as fast as possible for Becca's sleepover, even though it
technically didn't begin till five. And I tried not to think

about Dad in his kayak, wondering why he isn't good enough for his own daughter.

I drop my bike under Becca's house and haul my overnight bag up the stairs. Cooper, the resident Lab at Polka Dot Books next door, barks and jumps with all of his doggy enthusiasm against the wooden fence.

"Hey, buddy." I hang over the railing on the top step and wave at him.

"Hey, buddy, yourself." Becca's opened the door. "Why are you here so early? Not that I mind, of course. I need someone who can com . . . comser . . ."

"Commiserate?" I suggest. It's been Lauren's word of the week, and I think we've all heard it in every possible way it can be used by now. Lauren's going to be single-handedly responsible for all of us acing the SAT in high school.

"Yeah, that," Becca says. She slumps against the door frame. "Because my life is over."

"Becs, they're only braces. I mean, yeah, you can't eat a few things, but it's not that horrible." I dump my bag inside the door, underneath the Sandpiper Beach Citizens of the Year awards honoring Becca's parents, and head straight for the kitchen. "And besides, this party is all about having one last blast, right? You'll eat

VI

so much of that stuff tonight, you won't be able to miss it for the next couple of years."

Becca trudges behind me. "It's not that. Well, maybe it is a little. But mostly it's my face! I'm gonna be a brace-face, and Philippe will never, ever, ever in a hundred million years find that cute."

"Philippe?" I stop in the middle of pulling out ingredients for caramel apples.

"He's just . . . really nice. And megacute. Don't give me that look! I *know* I swore off boys. It doesn't really even matter now, does it? Plus we have school pictures next week, remember? So when I'm fifty and trying to recapture my youth by looking at my seventh-grade picture, all I'll remember is braces."

Poor Becca looks so upset. I give her a hug. Then I hand her a bag of caramel candy to unwrap. "Put that in a bowl so we can melt it, okay? I promise cooking will make you feel better. It always works for me. I baked a pile of muffins this morning. Which means we've got breakfast for tomorrow." I nod toward my backpack in the living room.

Becca slowly unwraps the caramels while she looks at me. "What happened? Did you run into Lance and Linney?"

Ugh. Why does *everyone* think everything has to do with Lance? "No. Wait, why would I have run into them together? Are they, like . . . boyfriend and girlfriend?"

Becca shrugs. "No, I don't think so. But she's been hanging out at Stewie's a lot. So if it isn't Lance, what's bothering you so much that you had to bake?"

I run water over a bunch of apples in the sink and start scrubbing them dry. I'm not really sure I want to talk about it. Becca would totally get it, of course. She was there for the whole awful puke scene, and she was even there when Dad announced he'd gotten the job at school. She looked about as horrified as I felt about that news.

But it's Becca's birthday party, and honestly, I don't really feel like talking about it. If I could go the rest of the night without thinking about that look on Dad's face, I'd feel a whole lot better.

"I don't really want to talk about it," I say.

So we make caramel apples, and I listen to Becca worry about how much the braces will hurt and whether anyone will call her names (which is crazy, really, since lots of girls in our class have already gotten braces) and whether she'll have the braces off before she's in high school and goes to prom and whether she should get all one color bands or mix it up with two or three.

By the time Sadie and Lauren arrive, we've not only got caramel apples; we've also got deep-dish pizza (Dr. Bernstein told Becca that the crust can damage her braces; who knew pizza crust was so dangerous?), saltwater taffy, bowls and bowls of every flavor of popcorn we could think of, sunflower seeds, and even beef jerky, which Becca said she was only going to eat because she wouldn't be allowed to eat it after Monday.

"Ooh, popcorn!" Lauren digs a hand into the nearest bowl. "I've been studying pretty much all day. I am *so* ready for this party!"

"Pizza! I'm starving." Sadie goes to grab a slice, and I have to smack both their hands away.

"Let's get it all upstairs first," I tell them. Becca's parents have a strict no-eating-in-your-bedroom rule, which totally makes sense since food could get lost really easily in Becca's room, but I guess Becca was so miserable that they decided to bend it for tonight.

Upstairs, we shove aside piles of clothes and school papers and things I can't identify (I swear I think I saw some squished papier-mâché we did in second grade). Then we eat and eat and eat. Becca wants to watch her favorite teen-romance movies, since, she says, "This stuff will never happen to me now." That just sounds way too depressing, so we talk her out of it and into dressing up and taking pictures instead. Which is So Very Becca.

"Then you won't care about your school pictures because you'll have these to look at instead!" Sadie says as Becca pulls on the fanciest dress she owns.

Lauren snaps shots of Becca sitting, Becca standing, Becca leaning mournfully against her closet door, Becca jumping up like a cheerleader, and Becca strumming her guitar. Sadie scooches across the floor to where I'm sitting.

"Something's up with you," she says.

I sigh. "It's Becca's party. I don't want to ruin it by being all grumpy."

"What happened?" Sadie's eyebrows are knitted together.

Now I have to tell her, or she'll assume someone died. "It's my dad. I asked him to quit, and it . . . didn't go like I planned." I rifle through Becca's jewelry box. I know she decided at Founder's Day to start collecting brooches, and I guess she's really committed. There are a ton of them in here. I push the old-fashioned pins aside and find a long beaded necklace to wind around my neck.

"Is he mad at you?"

"No, but I think I really hurt his feelings. I just feel so . . . awful. And mean. My dad's always been there for me, and I was so horrible to him. Now he thinks I'm embarrassed by him, and that he's not good enough, and officially, I am the worst daughter who ever existed."

Sadie leans over and wraps me in a bear hug. "I totally get it," she says.

Wait, she does. Sadie said she's still going out of her way not to bring up any wedding talk around her mom because it always gets awkward.

"Um, helloooo?" Becca's snapping her fingers. "No whispering! It's group-shot time! Vi, you put on that red velvet dress. Sades, you need the faux-fur-trimmed coat. It'll look *très* cute on you! And someone needs to wear these adorbs gold sandals!" She scoops the shoes up and tosses them to Lauren, who falls back into a mountain of clothing as she catches them.

Sadie giggles, and I can't help smiling.

I'm pulling on the hem of the dress to try to make it longer (because Becca is shrimp-size and I'm what she once called "statuesque"), and Lauren's wrapping a hot pink scarf around her neck (I might not be the fashion queen of Sandpiper Beach, but even I get that a scarf doesn't really go with sandals), when Sadie's phone rings with the RSVP theme song that Becca wrote this summer.

La la la la la la la la, life is so much more . . .

Sadie freezes mid–camera shot.

"Maybe it's just Izzy," I suggest.

"Or someone who's heard about the awesomeness of RSVP and wants to book a party," Becca adds. "Of course, we'll have to turn them down like the others, though." We'd agreed after we booked the wedding that it was all the party planning we could handle with school and stuff.

La la la la la la la la, shared among us four . . .

"Or your mom, calling to remind you about something," Lauren says.

Sadie pulls the phone from her purse on the floor and glances at the screen. Her shoulders sag. "It's her," she announces before she puts the phone to her ear. "Hello, Miss Worthington?"

"This woman is way more trouble than this wedding is worth. Seriously, we'd make more money if we quit, because then we could book other parties. You know, for normal people," Lauren whispers.

"Shh!" I say to her. If that bridezilla can hear Lauren, we'll get kicked off the wedding for sure. And getting fired isn't exactly great for business.

"But it's true! I can prove it. See, I have this spreadsheet that logs how much time we're putting into this wedding and then calculates what our hourly rate would be based on the total amount of payment she's offered us, and—"

Sadie kicks at Lauren's leg.

"Ow!" Lauren hops up and down on one gold-sandaled foot.

"I see, Miss Worthington, but . . ." Sadie slumps onto Becca's bed. "How about tomorrow morning? . . . Oh . . . No, of course we want to do everything we can, but right now we're . . ."

I sit next to her. I'm dying to know what Miss Worthington is talking about. I poke Sadie's leg. *What?* I mouth. *What's she saying?*

Sadie waves a hand at me. "Yes, we still want the job! . . . No, I understand. . . . Okay, thirty minutes. See you then." Sadie clicks her phone off and falls backward onto the bed.

"What was *that* all about?" Becca asks.

"Bridezilla emergency. She's found some guy called 'the Italian Tenor' she wants to sing at the wedding, but he's only available to Skype with us about predicted wedding-day humidity conditions that could affect his vocal cords tonight, because then he's heading off on the Australian leg of his world tour. Please ask me if I understood more than six words of the sentence I just said." Sadie pushes herself up onto her elbows. "The part I got loud and clear is that she wants one of us at her house. Right now."

Sadie

9

TODAY'S TO-DO LIST:
- [ ] google "ways to deal with bridezillas"
- [ ] figure out what an Italian Tenor is
- [ ] appoint a vice president to deal with all this stuff from now on

$\mathcal{S}$o when she says right now, she means—" Becca starts.

"Right *now*!" I cut in.

"But, but, but . . . it's my birthday party! Did you tell her that?"

I shake my head, sigh, and gather my hair into a ponytail. Time to get down to business. Literally. I slide off Becca's faux-fur coat and scrub at the glitter she applied to my cheeks earlier. Nothing says unprofessional like glitter cheeks!

As the tiny sparkles disappear, my sparkly mood does too. I'd been soooo looking forward to tonight. A sleepover with my very best friends was supposed to have been the perfect way to escape all the stress of this stupid wedding and the awkwardness of things at home. Mom's been acting like her normal self, distracted but Mom-ish, although she *has* been around an awful lot, which is actually not normal (yesterday she and Izzy played Monopoly for approximately three hours). But whenever anything about her party-planning company *or* mine comes up, the air gets chillier than the ice-cream freezer at the Variety Shoppe.

And speaking of my company, it really does feel like mine most days, with all the responsibility that comes with that. I know RSVP belongs to all of us, but I'm the president and I'm the one whose cell-phone number is on all our flyers, which means *I'm* the one getting each and every "Sadie-babe, I was thinking" phone call from Alexandra Worthington. And there are a lot of "Sadie-babe, I was thinking" phone calls. It's like the woman is incapable of making a decision and sticking to it.

Plus *everything* is urgent. Everything. Like two days ago when we had to figure out right away if the birdseed that people would be throwing on her and Ike instead of rice as they left the ceremony could be a diet variety because she'd noticed all the seagulls around Sandpiper Beach seemed fat and she didn't want to contribute to the Great Gull Obesity Epidemic.

And now I'm gonna have to miss half of Becca's party all because *I'm* the one in charge. I'm so totally over it.

Next to me, Vi is tugging a pair of sweats on under her too-short Becca dress. "Wait up," she says. "I'll come with."

I smile at her, grateful for the offer even though I'm guessing it has every bit as much to do with being able to take off the tiny dress.

"I can't believe y'all are really going!" Becca cries. "This mega stinks. Queen Alexandra needs to know there are limits! What if you just told her you were stuck somewhere important? Like, um, the hospital, or something." Becca's voice is getting high-pitched as she tosses clothes from her bed, looking for a place to sit. Finally she gives up and plops down on top of a pile of sweaters.

I puff my bangs out of my eyes and tug the laces on my sneakers. "She knows I'm not, Becs. I just told her I was on my way. Besides, she'd probably just fire us or something, and then my mom would know we couldn't hack it as wedding planners. No way am I letting that happen. Although I *am* starting to get a new appreciation for all the times Mom's had to skip out on us for bride stuff, that's for sure."

"But it's already dark out!" Now Becca's voice is getting whiny. I love the girl to pieces, but it's hard not to get annoyed when she whines. It's not like leaving is my choice. At all.

Lauren peers out Becca's window. "It is pretty pitch-black out there, Sades."

I know. I know all of these things. But I still have to go when duty calls. Isn't that what being president is all about? Now I get why Dad used to say you couldn't pay him enough to run for mayor. Responsibility kinda stinks.

Vi grabs her sweatshirt with one hand and my arm with the other. "We'll be fine. We'll stick together. Besides, it's Sandpiper Beach. What's gonna happen?"

Lauren lets Becca's curtain fall back in front of the window and sighs a big, deep sigh. "A one-point-oh-three-percent crime rate is still not zero. It'll be way faster and safer if I drive you there, Sades. Her house has to be a half mile away."

The three of us stare at her with our jaws *thisclose* to the floor. Vi finds her voice first. "But, Lo, you aren't allowed to drive anyone in your golf cart. Wouldn't your parents kill you?"

Becca smiles sweetly. "They didn't find out when Lauren gave *me* a ride this summer."

Vi and I jerk our heads to Lauren. "For real?" I ask.

Lauren shrugs and studies the carpet. "It was just one time. Before the Scottish party. She needed to buy too much stuff to carry in her bike basket."

Becca laughs. "And it was totally awesome. The wind in our hair. The pavement under our wheels. The boys staring at us as we breezed past. I'm totes cut out for convertible living."

Lauren balls up her sweater and lobs it at Becca before saying, "I'm one hundred percent committed to my schedule, and this party is my fun time. So if we have to answer Miss Worthington's annoying call, the least we can do is have a blast getting there and back, right? Besides, the faster we go, the faster we're back."

"Fabu!" says Becca. "Mani-pedis will be waiting. Hey, Vi, change out of those icky sweats and back into something fun. I'll fill the tub so we can stick our feet in and soften our cuticles. Ooh, and if you don't want that dress again, try these leggings. They have rhine-stones!"

Becca holds up the twinkling pants as Vi looks at me and Lauren with a *Help me* expression on her face. I can't help but laugh. I can practically see the little thought bubble over her head that says *Rhinestone leggings are So Not Vi!*, but she laughs and plops down next to Becca on the bed.

"Don't leave me with Becs too long, y'all. By the time you get back, I'll probably have orange streaks in my hair."

Becca whacks Vi over the head with a pillow. "You will *not*. Besides, you're a summer, coloring-wise. I'd never recommend orange for you. Now, if you want a nice shade of rose, periwinkle, or sage, we should talk. . . ."

Lauren and I duck out, leaving the other two to their sleepover fun. Halfway down the stairs, we can hear Becca's mom chatting away on the phone. When we get to the bottom, I turn toward the kitchen to let Mrs. Elldridge know where we're headed. We wait in the doorway, but she's so involved in her conversation, she doesn't even turn our way.

Lauren tugs on my sleeve. "Come on, let's just go.

We'll be back soon anyway. And Becca and Vi can tell her where we've gone."

I raise my eyebrows. "Who are you and what happened to Lauren?" She's probably the last person I'd ever think of bending the rules.

She gives me a nervous smile. "I'm supposed to be having fun between the hours of five and eleven thirty tonight. At exactly eleven thirty, my phone will beep to remind me to go to sleep. So let's make the most of it, okay? If we hang around here waiting, it'll take us longer to get there, and we'll have less time for the party."

I look back at Becca's mom just as she disappears into the pantry. Lauren's right; we need to get going. Plus, Miss Worthington will be mad if we take too long getting there.

We slip quietly out through the front door. Even though she's hiding it well, I can tell Lauren is nervous about the whole driving-people-in-her-golf-cart thing, because she's extra quiet as we slip down the stairs to the spot under the house where it's parked.

"Sure you're okay with this?" I ask one last time as we climb onto the bench seat.

"It'll be fun. And it's the most logical solution,"

Lauren answers. When it comes to Lauren and logic, there's no arguing, so I close my mouth.

We pull out onto the dark streets. Even in the months when we don't have to worry about artificial lights causing the baby sea turtles to get confused and head away from the ocean, Sandpiper Beach is so small and quiet that streetlights would ruin the "ambiance" (or so Mom has said). Only the public places and a few businesses, like the square and the marina, have them. On nights without a moon, like tonight, it's so dark you can barely see the shapes of the houses lining the streets, unless they're lit up from the inside. Cooper gives a small woof from the porch of Polka Dot Books as we drive away from Becca's.

We turn down Sandpiper Drive and onto Pelican Street. Lauren is concentrating on navigating the dark streets, and I don't want to bother her, so I breathe in the smell of the salt water and listen for the crashing waves. The air is eerily still, and there's the tiniest hint of crispness to it, which makes me shiver happily. I love October the best, and not just because of Halloween.

Except, speaking of Halloween, Becca's been suspiciously quiet about her costume plans for us, and it's almost here. She always gets us to coordinate costumes.

Last year it was the Four Musketeers (we added one we called Sadoths to match Porthos, Athos, and Aramis) and the year before that we were the Wicked Witch of the West, the Tin Man, the Scarecrow, and Dorothy. Three guesses who insisted on wearing the sparkly red shoes!

I angle my knees toward Lauren. "Hey, is Becca still being super-secretive about her costume ideas for—" Before I can finish, an engine revs behind us, and the entire golf cart lights up with flashing red-and-blue lights. My heart takes a ride on the Tower of Terror all the way into my shoes. (Not red. Not sparkly.)

Lauren stands on the brake, and we both jerk forward, then slam back against the seat. The golf cart skids to a stop in the middle of Pelican Street while the police cruiser crunches gravel as it rolls close, then parks a few feet away. A car door closes. I'm too scared to look at Lauren, so I turn in my seat and squint at Officer Davis as he approaches.

He aims a flashlight right into our faces, and I blink hard to keep my eyes from watering.

"That you, Sadie Pleffer? And Lauren Simmons?"

Lauren recovers her eyesight—and her voice—first and answers a quiet "Yes, sir."

"You girls out for a joyride or something?" Officer

Davis asks, shining the beam of light all around the golf-cart floor and into its back storage space.

"We, um, we were just on our way to a meeting with a client, sir," I offer. I still don't want to look at Lauren, because she must be totally freaking out, and I'm scared that if I see that, I will too.

"A client?" By the light of the flashing bar on top of the cruiser's roof, I can see Officer Davis's eyebrows hitch up. "Oh, that's right. You girls doing that birthday party thing these days, ain't ya? Planned my niece Molly's party this summer at the Plantation House. I heard all about that murder mystery you gals done up. First murder ever recorded at Sandpiper Beach, proud to say. And a fake one, at that. Molly had herself a right good time."

I nod, and out of the corner of my eye I see Lauren do the same. When he doesn't say anything next, I decide he must want more from us.

"We're doing a wedding now, sir. And, um, the bride, well, she insisted we meet with her tonight about something. It's really important."

"Thing is, girls, I wonder if y'all know the laws regarding operating vehicles on the road at night without any headlights."

I gulp, and Lauren makes this tiny squeaking noise

in her throat. "No, sir," I answer. "But, um, it's just a golf cart, not really a vehicle."

Lauren sinks into her seat. I know she's wishing I would just be quiet already, and I want to. I do. But I'm so freaked out, my mouth doesn't seem connected to my brain.

"Got four wheels and an engine, don't it?" Officer Davis asks. "Makes it a vehicle in my book. And Judge Athens's book too, I might add."

Another noise from Lauren, and I reach over to grab her hand. My palms are so sweaty I doubt it helps calm her down, though.

"This your daddy's *vehicle*, Lauren?"

Lauren nods, completely silent.

"He can pick it up first thing in the morning, if he wants. Should be fine here till then. I need you to pull it on over to the side, please. Then I'm afraid I'm goin' have to ask you to step out of the vehicle and hop into the backseat of my cruiser."

In the backseat of his police car? Like, where criminals sit? Omigosh, are we getting arrested?

Lauren drives into the sandy grass on the shoulder and flips the switch to power down the golf cart. When she gets out, her legs look all wobbly. I slide across the bench and step out next to her. My legs hold, but my stomach is feeling super twisty as I follow Lauren to Officer Davis's car. There's an acid taste in my mouth, and I'm worried I might throw up.

The policeman holds open the back door, and I duck my head and step in behind Lauren. Metal bars separate the front seat from the back. Officer Davis gets into the driver's seat and turns off the flashing lights. Having the red-and-blue lights go away makes me feel a tiny bit better, but I still don't know what's gonna happen now. Is he taking us to *jail*?

In the dark Lauren finds my hand and squeezes. Hard. When I peer at her face, her eyes are wide and round, and I can see she's just as freaked out as I am. My poor friend who never even jaywalks is sitting in the back of a police car, all because of me and my stupid jumping-whenever-Alexandra-Worthington-commands. I have to get us out of this.

"Um, sir," I ask, and I can't even believe how shaky my voice sounds, "are we under arrest?"

My shoulders drop in relief when he laughs.

"Arrest? For driving without headlights in a golf cart? Shoot, no. I couldn't just leave you there in the dark. Don't know why you'd know this, but our crime rate is only 1.03 percent here on Sandpiper Beach. Even so, still never pays to take any chances. I'll run you by the station and Officer Rodriguez'll ring up your parents to come fetch you."

Our parents. I guess I knew this wouldn't end without them finding out about it, but hearing Officer Davis say it makes it feel so much more real. My mom is going to kill me. Lauren's mom is going to extra kill her. Not only is she driving the golf cart at night, but she had me in there with her, which is a huge no-no and Lauren knows it. And we'll probably get Becca in trouble, since we didn't tell her mom that we were leaving.

I let my head fall back against the seat as we creep toward the station. Next to me Lauren is quiet, but her hand is squeezing mine tighter than ever, and I'm betting she's willing herself not to cry. I really, really, *really* wish I'd just walked there with Vi when she'd offered.

In the quiet and the dark, my cell phone springs to life with the ringtone for RSVP. Becca's voice singing "Ordinary Tuesdays" doesn't make me smile the way it usually does. Not even a little bit. I can only *imagine* the angry voice mail Alexandra Worthington is leaving right now, but even that is nothing compared to the lecture I'm about to get from Mom. Greeee*aaaat*.

10

Lauren

remorse noun \ ri-ˈmȯrs \
a feeling of being sorry; a feeling of guilt over having
done wrong
Use in a sentence:
I am full of remorse for driving Sadie in the golf
cart at night, getting picked up by the police, and
disappointing Mom and Dad.

I've been in trouble with my parents exactly five and a
half times in my life, not including stuff I might've done
before I could remember, like flushing my toddler toothbrush down the toilet. But none of those five and a half
times were for anything worse than hiding Josh's football
equipment when he refused to play with me, or accidentally breaking Dad's favorite boat statue-thing when the
girls and I were trying to do cartwheels in the living room.

This is way, way, way worse than any of that. And it's all because I decided that since I'm studying extra hard, I should also be having the most fun I can during those slots on my schedule. It sounded logical at the time, but now? I'm not so sure.

"Do you girls want some more hot chocolate?" Officer Rodriguez asks. "I'm sorry we don't have any marshmallows. My kids always like lots of marshmallows in their hot chocolate."

We shake our heads. Sadie's barely touched hers, and mine isn't really sitting all that well in my stomach, because I can't stop thinking about how my parents are going to react to canceling their date night in Wilmington to come pick up their juvenile-delinquent daughter. Mom's probably already crying.

I don't know what I thought was going to happen when we got to the police station, but it definitely wasn't this. When we walked in, Sadie and I were so nervous that we had to hold on to each other. She kept apologizing to me, which is silly because I'm the one who offered to drive her. But I was so scared—and so angry at myself—that I couldn't say anything until about ten minutes ago.

We had to sit in these hard plastic chairs by his desk

while Officer Rodriguez called our parents. After he made the calls, he told us to sit on the comfiest couch that's probably ever existed. Then he brought us blankets, made us hot chocolate, and rolled in a little TV on a wheeled cart. He put the TV on a cartoon channel, which is hilarious, because he has four kids, all under six years old. He's probably forgotten that anything besides cartoons even exists on TV. This is all really nice considering we've broken the law and everything.

The police station is a lot quieter than I thought it would be too. But then again, this is Sandpiper Beach, with practically no crime. I suppose a police station in, say, Raleigh or New York would be a lot busier, with phones ringing off the hook and criminals coming in and stuff. Sandpiper Beach's police station is just one room with some potted plants, a few framed pictures of the beach, this couch, the awful chairs, and a couple of desks. And hot chocolate.

"Are you hungry? We've got some cans of soup back in the break room." Officer Rodriguez stands, ready to spring into soup-making action. It's not like that 1.03 percent crime rate means he gets to spring into action all that often.

"No, thank you," Sadie replies. I shake my head in

agreement. I couldn't eat anything right now. Not while I'm waiting for my parents to arrive in a storm of confusion and anger and worst of all . . . disappointment.

Officer Rodriguez sits back down, looking very dadlike and worried.

"I hope your mom gets here first," I say quietly to Sadie.

Sadie reaches over and squeezes my hand. Her phone buzzes again—the fourth time since we got here—but she doesn't even look at it this time. We both know it's Alexandra Worthington, and I know Sadie's not really in the mood to explain what's going on. "She'll just think we got held up somewhere," she says when the phone finally stops buzzing.

And that's when I finally notice the worry that's taken over Sadie's face. She keeps chewing on her bottom lip, and her eyebrows are doing that scrunching thing. Maybe I can stop stressing about myself for two minutes and do something to help my friend.

"Here." I reach over and pluck Sadie's phone from her lap. I pull up her text messages and start typing.

"What are you doing?" she asks.

"Dealing with a little of this wedding stress for you." I show her the message I've just sent to Miss Worthington.

Major emergency just came up. Can't come by tonight. Pls call Becca regarding the Singing Spaniard. (910) 555-1541.

"You're welcome," I fill in when Sadie doesn't say anything. I can tell she's waffling between relief and a total meltdown about not being in complete control over everything. "Becs and Vi can handle it. Since, you know, they're not looking at a future in juvie or anything." Just saying that makes my heart twitch. I really hope Officer Rodriguez was right when he said none of this was going down on our permanent records. I know—I made sure to ask him, even before he called our parents. It was about the only intelligible thing I could say at that point. Intelligible: able to be understood or comprehended.

I type out a quick message to Becca—AW calling you in 3, 2, 1 . . .—before handing the phone back to Sadie. "It'll be okay," I say, when she still doesn't say anything. "She won't fire us over this. Not if she hasn't because of anything else yet."

Sadie's eyebrows scrunch together even more under her bangs. "It's not that. It's . . . Lauren, he's the *Italian Tenor*! Not the Singing Spaniard."

That's what she's worried about? We're waiting for our

parents to get us from the *police station*, and Sadie's freaking out over me calling this singer guy by the wrong name?

She's flipping her phone around in her hands, and I realize that she's super nervous about everything too—being here, having her mom called, whether Miss Worthington really is going to fire us this time, not to mention whether her mom actually is okay about us handling this wedding—and that fixating on this one little detail is her way of dealing with it.

I'm about to say something when the door to the station flies open.

This is it. D-Day. The Rapture. The end of the world. Or, really, worse than any of those if it's my parents coming through that door. I clutch Sadie again as we wait to see who it is.

The quiet whine of a motor filters through the room, followed by a series of bumps and thumps, and a few not-so-nice words.

Bubby?

My heart about leaps out of my chest. I know that's entirely impossible, since one's heart is firmly planted in the chest cavity, but that's what it feels like. It's not Mom or Dad come to give me disappointed eyes, but Bubby.

"Mrs. Simmons?" Officer Rodriguez stands up at

his desk again. "Ma'am, I don't think you can fit that in here. Let me help you." He moves toward the door.

"Please, Diego Rodriguez. I've known you since you trotted around town in your Spider-Man costume for a whole year. You can call me Gerry. Or Bubby. Everyone does." Bubby giggles. She *giggles*. Then Wanda bumps the door frame again, and Bubby utters one more choice word outside the door before she revs Wanda's motor. The sound of it disappears as the door shuts. Officer Rodriguez opens the door again.

"You can park it right there, ma'am," he says. "That's the captain's spot, but he's not here tonight."

"Is that *Bubby*?" Sadie finally whispers.

I nod. "I think so."

"Let me help you, ma—I mean, Bubby." Officer Rodriguez disappears from view and returns a minute later with Bubby on his arm.

Bubby's smiling like she's coming to collect me from a victorious It's All Academic meet, not at the police station because I've been picked up for reckless golf-cart driving.

She wiggles her fingers at me, beauty-queen style. "Hey-o, my LoLo!"

"Hi, Bubby . . ." is about all I can manage. She's not

mad, that's for sure. She probably thinks this is some exciting adventure.

Bubby takes the hard plastic seat that Officer Rodriguez pulls out for her.

"Would you like some coffee? Water? I think I've got some Cheerwine in the fridge," Officer Rodriguez says. He's probably about ready to make Bubby some soup, too. Somehow I think he likes having company, even if that company remembers every embarrassing thing he did as a kid.

"That's so kind of you," Bubby says. "But let's get down to business. How much to spring my granddaughter from this joint? What's the bail?" She opens her purse and drops a pile of bills on the desk.

Sadie's mouth flops open. I think mine does too. Who knew Bubby toted around so much money?

Officer Rodriguez stares at the cash for a moment. It's probably more than he makes hanging out here with us. Then he shakes his head. "Oh, no, Mrs.—Bubby. Lauren was just driving the golf cart without a headlight. That's all."

"I see." Bubby tucks the money back into her purse. "And she gave you the four-one-one without a lawyer present?"

Officer Rodriguez laughs. A little nervously, I think. "She's not under arrest. We just didn't want the girls driving home in the dark."

Bubby stares him down for a moment. Then her face changes completely—she smiles and bats her eyelashes. "Well then, I so totes appreciate you taking care of my Lo Baby and Sadie." She stands up and reaches out to touch his arm.

I bite my lip to keep from either laughing or throwing up. Sadie smothers a giggle behind her hand.

"Now give me the dish," Bubby's saying to Officer Rodriguez as she snakes her arm around his. "Did the girls sign anything while they were here? Any kind of . . . confession, perhaps?"

Officer Rodriguez glances down at his arm, which is imprisoned by Bubby's. He's looking just a tiny bit uncomfortable, poor guy. "No, ma'am. I just need a parent or guardian to take these girls home."

Bubby rewards him with a tinkling laugh.

"Can I go home with you?" Sadie whispers. "I'd rather play pinochle with Bubby than face my mom."

What Sadie doesn't realize is that Bubby is the calm before the storm of my parents. "Bunco," I say. "Bubby likes Bunco." Because that makes sense to say right now.

"Well, you see, Officer Diego Hotriguez—you don't mind if I call you that, do you? It's just so fitting." Bubby doesn't even seem to notice that Officer Rodriguez is flushing more than anyone thought possible. "My son and his wife are on their way back from Wilmington, and they called and asked me to pick Lo up and take her home. Now, that won't be any problem, will it? Has anyone ever told you that you have the nicest eyelashes? They're so long and . . . eyelashy." Bubby gives him her most winning smile.

Sadie buries her face in my shoulder as she shakes with laughter. I'd probably be laughing more if I could stop thinking about my parents cutting their date night short and driving home right now.

Officer Rodriguez gives a nervous cough and makes a halfhearted effort to pull his arm away from Bubby, who's holding on way too tight. "Um, of course you can take her home," he says, probably dying to get her off him and out of the station. "Just let me call her parents first to make sure."

"Fab!" she says. "Do I need to sign anything? And can you tell me about expungement? I don't want this little incident going down on my Lo's permanent record. She's going to Harvard, you know."

I'm not at all sure where I want to go to college yet, but Bubby's compliment makes me go warm all over. And then cold. Will my future college *know* I got hauled into the police station for driving without a headlight?

"Oh no, of course not," Officer Rodriguez says. "There's no record or anything."

I lean back against the couch with a sigh. At least something is going right.

"Why, that's just the bee's knees," Bubby says as she gives Officer Rodriguez's arm a little pat.

"Now if you'll just let me . . ." He pulls his arm again.

Bubby giggles. She lets go, but only to stand on her tiptoes and plant a kiss on his cheek. "Thank you for being such a dear."

Officer Rodriguez is lobster red. He rubs his arm, and it takes him a moment to find his voice. "Let me, uh, make that call."

I lean over and hug Sadie. "Good luck," I tell her.

"Text me and let me know how your parents take it," she says.

"If you don't hear from me, I'm probably confined to my room with bread and water." I stand up and join Bubby at the door. Officer Rodriguez joins us after he hangs up with my parents.

"Now, don't you worry, Diego Hotriguez," she says. "I have an extra-bright headlight on ol' Wanda here."

"But two people can't fit on that. Are y'all walking back home?" Officer Rodriguez rubs the back of his neck. "It's a little late."

"Oh no, no. I got Mr. Wheeler to drive us. He was just dying to take me out for a spin in his Caddy." Bubby waves at an enormous car parked at the end of the lot. A tiny old man in the driver's seat waves back. "Now, why don't you show me how strong you are and put ol' Wanda into the backseat, Officer Hotriguez?"

I'm curled up on our boat-patterned armchair, arms wrapped around my knees, while Mom sits stiffly on the couch. Dad's gone to make coffee. I guess they need caffeine in order to handle this situation, even though it's almost ten o'clock. Mr. Wheeler drove Bubby back to Sandpiper Active Senior Living just a few minutes ago, right after Mom and Dad got home.

And now I'm really in for it.

I'm probably the only person I know who's never been grounded. That's not so hard to accomplish when you've got brothers like mine, who require Mom and Dad's constant disciplinary attention. Accidentally breaking a statue was barely even a blip on their radar. Somehow I think I might ruin my perfect record tonight. Why did I let myself go so crazy with the having fun thing, again?

Dad comes back into the living room with two mugs (one with a sailboat, the other with a paddlewheel steamboat) for him and Mom. I rest my chin on my knees and brace myself for one of the scenes I've over-heard between them and Zach.

Mom takes a sip of coffee, sets it on the table, and then places her hands on her legs. She's still in her going-out clothes—nice black dress with a sparkly red sweater, and heels. Her dark curly hair frames her tired face. "I don't know where to start," she finally says. "I'd say that we're disappointed in you, but mostly we're just confused. We'd expect something like this from your brothers, but not you."

Well, that's new. Usually I think they're just waiting for me to turn into Zach or Josh. Wait, this isn't good. Maybe now I'm proving them right.

"How about we start with: What in the world were you thinking?" Dad asks.

I pull my hands into the sleeves of my sweatshirt and take a deep breath. "It was a business emergency."

Maybe if I frame it that way, they'll understand. I mean, Dad runs his own business, and Mom is constantly on call at the hospital.

Mom raises her eyebrows. Dad sighs and crosses his arms over his belly in its yacht-embroidered polo shirt. My parents are like night and day—Mom all neat and pulled together, Dad a boat-patterned mess.

They don't say anything, so I go on. "Our wedding client called and insisted someone come over right away to talk to the Spanish Crooner or something. She pretty much said if we didn't, then she'd have to find another planner for her wedding. Vi was going to walk over there with Sadie, but Miss Worthington's house is all the way down by the beach. I was worried about them walking there in the dark. Because of crime and . . . wild animals, you know?" I cringe as the words come out of my mouth. The most wild animal that exists on Sandpiper Beach is the seagull, whose scariest attack moment is stealing the lunch right out of your hands on the beach.

"And?" Mom prompts.

I twist my sleeve-covered hands together. I'm not about to tell them that I thought driving Sadie there would be fun. "So I offered to drive Sadie. We were just going to be there a few minutes." I have no idea if this is true, but I don't know that it's not true either. "And then we were going to head right back to Becca's house."

"And it didn't occur to you to ask Becca's parents for a ride?" Dad asks.

"I, uh, no?" That's such an obvious solution. Why in the world didn't we think of that?

"Or tell this woman to wait until the morning?" Mom adds.

"She wouldn't wait," I explain.

"I think I need to have a word with her. Expecting twelve-year-old girls to go out after dark to cater to her every whim . . . what nerve." Mom grips her mug, and I can tell she's just itching to tell Alexandra Worthington where to get off. Which makes me both happy and scared at the same time. I've been having doubts about her, but RSVP *can't* be fired as her client. But, then again, Sadie and I are both in huge trouble because of her.

"What I don't understand—and there are several things I don't understand about this entire situation—is why you and Sadie left without even saying a word to Becca's parents. Lauren, you *know* better than that," Dad says.

His words sting. Because I do know better than that. I was just so focused on making the most of my six and a half hours of fun that I didn't want to waste even a second. Somehow I don't think Mom and Dad will accept that as an answer, though.

Mom sets her mug on the table. "I cannot believe Bubby just had to pick you up at the police station. I doubt she's even been to the police station before. I'm embarrassed, Lauren."

I am too. Although I think Bubby actually enjoyed herself.

"After all the stunts Josh and Zach pulled, we never got a call from the police about either one of them," Dad says.

Well, that might still happen, but I don't point that out. I'm also pretty sure both Zach and Josh have done stuff that would have ended in a call from the police if they'd been caught. But I don't say that, either.

Really, there's only one thing I can say in this situation to try to dig myself out. It's all truth, so I sit up straight and let it out. "I'm so sorry about all of this. You're right that I should've thought the whole thing through before Sadie and I left. I know you're going to ask me to quit RSVP, but I can't do that. This wedding is way too big for Sadie, Vi, and Becca to pull off without me. Although sometimes I think maybe we should drop Miss Worthington, because it's not like we're actually making money with the amount of time we spend on her. But, anyway, that's not the point. The point is that I need to refocus on my priorities. And I'm going to do that, starting right now." I curl my fingers under my legs as I finish the speech and wait for Mom and Dad's reactions.

"Lauren, honey, we weren't going to ask you to quit your business," Dad says.

"Although you and your friends might reconsider this Miss Worthington as a client," Mom adds. "Now, what are these priorities?"

Even though it should be obvious, I fill them in. "Doing exceptionally well in school and my extracurriculars so that I can get into a really great college. I won't get any more Bs. Working at the marina so I can save more money. And working with RSVP. That's all. No more video games with Zach or watching TV. Oh, and I completely understand if you feel the need to ground me."

Mom and Dad look at each other. I have no idea why they're not nodding in approval or agreeing that I'm making the responsible decision.

"Well, you are grounded," Mom says.

"Although it sounds as if you've grounded yourself," Dad says.

I'm not sure how refocusing on my priorities in life is the same as grounding. Truthfully, I should cut out RSVP, too, but I can't let my friends down. I already made the commitment to help them with this wedding. Also, helping to run a business will look really (really, really) good on my college applications.

"We just want you to use your head, Lauren," Mom says.

They should know that I'm perfectly capable of using my head. I'm not my brothers. Although I suppose they have to say that, since I *did* make a really dumb decision. Which will never happen again.

"If this Miss Worthington asks you to go out late at night or do anything else you know we'd disapprove of, you need to tell us. Okay?" she finishes.

I nod.

"No more calls from the police. Ever," Dad adds.

"Of course," I say. As if I'd ever want to relive *that* again. "So . . . what exactly does this grounding mean?" I ask carefully. I need to text Sadie and find out how everything went with her mom.

"No cell phone, no computer, no TV for a week," Mom recites as if she's said this a hundred times before. Which she probably has, for my brothers. "You go to school and the marina, and then you come straight home. And definitely no driving that golf cart. We'll have to discuss *that* later."

"But how will I talk to my friends about RSVP stuff? And my day planner."

"They can call you the old-fashioned way." Dad points to the (boat-shaped) landline phone resting on a side table. "Or you can talk to them at school. We'll print out your planner."

"How will I do my homework? I need my laptop for that." This grounding thing is lot a more complicated than I thought it would be.

"We have a perfectly fine computer in the kitchen you can use," Mom says.

I cringe. That computer is so ancient, I could take a shower in the amount of time it takes to boot up. "What about Halloween?"

Dad frowns, and I know he's thinking twice about making me miss Halloween. Not only is there trick-or-treating—which I admit I'm getting a little too old for—but there's a party at the pavilion by the beach, complete with a costume contest, a monster-mash dance, and even bobbing for apples. It's like Charlie Brown's Halloween come to life. And Becca's parents lead a ghost tour of all the supposedly haunted places on the island. Which is *not* something I'd be attending (I don't do ghosts), but still.

"Lauren?" Mom asks. "Did you hear me? No Halloween."

I nod. "Can I call Sadie? I want to make sure she's okay."

"Not right now," Dad says. "I'm sure she's fine, and she's probably having the same talk with her mom."

"And the house phone is *only* to be used for your business," Mom says. "Not for chitchatting with your friends."

As if I "chitchat." Okay, maybe I do. Sometimes. But not anymore. Chitchatting Lauren is going the same way as dancing Lauren and video-game-playing Lauren. I suppose I deserve it, though. Besides having to use the dinosaur computer and losing my phone, this grounding thing's not so bad, though. With my new focus on the things that matter, I won't be watching TV anyway. And the only places I need to go are to school and the marina. I'm sure my friends can cover any business-related trips for a week.

"Will you call Becca's mom and let her know that Sadie and I aren't coming back to the party?" I ask. Mostly, I don't want Becca and Vi to worry about us.

"Already done," Mom says.

"I feel as if we should say this will never happen again," Dad says.

"Of course it won't," I reply.

"Right," he says.

Mom and Dad follow me upstairs to collect my computer. I delete all of the "fun" reminders from my phone and hand that over to them too. After they leave, I drop onto my bed and stare at the ceiling. It's white, like the rest of my room. And there's not a single boat-related thing in here. It's like my refuge from my family.

After everything that's happened tonight, I feel weirdly calm. Almost good, actually. Like maybe I was trying to do too much before. And now that I've decided to cut out all of the unnecessary stuff, I'll have more time what's important—school and getting into the right college.

Nothing else.

Rate the Cake!

Rank each item on a scale from one to five hearts
(one heart is "blech" and five hearts is "super scrumptious!")

Name: Vi

Cake Flavor: dark chocolate peanut butter

Appearance: ♥♥♥♥♥ Like it just came from a fancy bakery in New York.

Texture: ♥♥ Kind of crumbly. (Texture can make or break a cake!)

Flavor: ♥♥♥♥♥ I need to get this recipe & add something to make it less crumbly. Pudding, maybe? Or applesauce?

Overall: ♥♥♥♥ YES!!!!!!! (But fix the crumbles.)

Name: Sadie

Cake Flavor: carrot

Appearance: ♥♥♥♥♥ Sooo pretty with the curled shredded carrot bits on top.

Texture: ♥♥ Spongy, which is weird but pretty good actually.

Flavor: ♥♥♥ I didn't expect the icing to be cream cheese! But it was still good.

Overall: ♥♥ I think this might not be the best choice for a wedding because it's not universally loved. Might be more practical to go with chocolate, which is a total crowd pleaser.

Name: Becca

Cake Flavor: raspberry lemon

Appearance: ♥♥♥♥♥ Looks delectable.

Texture: OUCH!

Flavor: OUCH!

Overall: DOUBLE OUCH!!!!!

Name: Lauren

Cake Flavor: ☹ Boo. We miss Lauren. Xoxo, Becca

Appearance:

Texture:

Flavor:

Overall:

Becca

~~Daily Love Horoscope for Scorpio:~~
Who cares. Who's gonna be interested in a
brace-face?

Owwwwwwwwwwwwwwwwwwwwwwwwwwwww.

No, seriously. OWW! Braces = lifetime of pain.

Lifetime, two years. Two years, lifetime. Same thing,
if you ask me. Also:

OWWWWWWWW!

I really, really, really, really, REALLY hate braces.
Really. It's only been two days and already I could start
a Museum of Gross Things with the little bits of gunk
I've pulled out of my cages. Whoever named the metal
brackets "cages" was so right-on, too. My pretty, shiny,

smooth teeth are totally caged in, like pearly zoo animals I'm not allowed to feed.

I hate this. It makes me want to laugh/cry that we spent the first half of my sleepover (the part *before* my two besties embarked on a crime spree and became juvenile delinquents) gorging ourselves on all the foods I wouldn't be able to eat with braces, like caramel apples and popcorn, but we didn't even consider mashed potatoes and mac 'n' cheese and Hershey's Kisses and string beans (what? They're good, even if they *are* veggies) and ruffled potato chips and meat loaf and basically ALL FOOD EVER. Because it hurts to eat *ev-er-y-thing*.

Mama says I should quit my whining and give it a couple of days, like Dr. Bernstein suggested, before making any snap judgments, but hello. Snap judgments are like gut feelings, and everyone says you should trust your gut feelings. Mine are saying I'm not even gonna be able to enjoy the wedding cake we're supposed to be sampling with Alexandra Worthington after school.

CAKE! Cake should always be happy. It's like a rule or something.

Oww.

I'm pacing the sidewalk outside Marks Makes Cakes because the last thing I want to do is run into Linney

Marks when I'm this cranky. I really abso-posi-lutely cannot be responsible for my actions in my current state. I debate wandering over to Merlin the Marlin since I'm stuck on some new song lyrics I'm working on and, for some weird reason, talking things through with an inanimate statue always helps. But then I spot Vi on her bike.

"I still can't get used to your new look," she says, once she's pulled up next to me.

I clamp my lips closed but . . . oww. Even that hurts, because I keep catching the inside of my lips on the stupid cages. I wish I could fall asleep like Snow White and wake up when it's time to get these things off. Except I'd have to bite into a poisoned apple for that to happen, and the thought of biting into any apple is . . . well, just . . . oww!

"Do you have the rating cards or does Sadie?" I ask. (Sadie thought it would be fun to rate each cake as we tasted, and she made up these cute little cards we could all use.) Only it comes out more like, "Oof oo ave oof ating ards oof oes adie?"

Vi tilts her head. "Huh?"

I use my fingers to unstick the inside of my lips from my braces and settle my top lip above the brackets. This is sooooo not gonna fly long-term. I repeat my question, but Vi is too busy giggling to hear me. She throws her arm around my shoulder and says, "Don't worry. They just take some getting used to."

Easy for her to say. *She* isn't the one who could fund a small war by melting the contents of *her* mouth.

Sadie rounds the corner next, swinging a shopping bag from one hand. She waves when she spots us. If anyone would know about dropping everything and running when a client calls, it's Mrs. Pleffer, but she was still pretty mad that Sadie left Becca's without telling a grown-up. So now Sadie's off screens for two weeks, but at least she can leave the house.

Technically, Lauren *could* be here too, because her parents said RSVP business was an exception, but she's auditioning for Poster Child of Grounding and figured she could earn extra brownie points by living a monk-like existence of school then homework followed by homework then school.

I love her to pieces, but she and I have polar-opposite viewpoints on grounding. I offered to give her survival tips since Mama and Daddy punish me for something practically every other day (example A: I just barely escaped losing screen privileges for allowing my friends to leave my sleepover without letting an adult know, even though it TOTES wasn't even *my* fault), but she wasn't interested.

Her loss.

Sadie turns to me with something that's halfway between a smile and a grimace. She's been following my braces saga pretty closely because at her last appointment Dr. Bernstein said he was still on the fence about whether she'd need them or not.

"Any better today?" she asks.

I make a face. "I managed applesauce for breakfast. It only hurt a medium amount."

Sadie looks horrified. "Oh. Um. Wow. I really hope it gets better soon. You're kind of scaring me."

I shrug and tuck my lyrics notebook into my purse. "I'm just telling it like it is, like any good friend would."

"Yes," says Vi. "We all know Becca would never exaggerate at all, ever. She's not the least bit melodramatic or anything."

Both my friends smile. Whatever. I'm too cranky to be a good sport about their teasing. "Should we go in?" I ask, holding the door for them.

The Markses' bakery smells like the North Pole married the *Nutcracker* suite—all buttercream frosting and gingerbread deliciousness. I fully expect the Sugar

Plum Fairy to pop out of the back room instead of Mrs. Marks. I for real don't understand how Linney could be so nasty when she grew up around so much sweet. (Luckily, I don't spot Girl Evil at all.)

We tried really extra hard to steer Alexandra away from having a traditional wedding cake alongside her dessert bar, just so we wouldn't have to deal with Linney, but since she couldn't be swayed, even I have to admit Linney's mom *does* have the best bakery in town. Maybe even anywhere.

"Hi, girls. Am I glad to see you! Your client is already here and was rather, um, insistent on inspecting my kitchen and offering some, er, suggestions. I'll let her know you're waiting!" Mrs. Marks's smile looks way too plastered on to be legit. Yikesies.

She waves her hand at metal chairs at a little cafe table tucked into the corner, and we're still figuring out how to cram around it when Alexandra appears, wiping her hands on a bright green Marks Makes Cakes apron she is, for some reason, wearing.

"You three are late!"

Sadie glances at the clock above the register. "Um, according to this, we're five minutes early, Miss Worthington."

"Precisely. Which is ten minutes late. All planners must be present and accounted for fifteen minutes prior to any scheduled meeting time. It's line item twenty-seven on the addendum to the contract I sent over last week."

Sadie squirms a little in her chair. "Sorry, ma'am. It won't happen again."

Alexandra slips her apron over her head and drops it across the cupcake display case. "Good. See that it doesn't. Now, I gave the bakery a few instructions for the décor I'd like to see on our cakes for today. She had some nonsense about not decorating the samples as we're just here to taste the flavors, but that's ridiculous. How will I know if I want real flowers or sugar flowers if I haven't seen them displayed for me? I was informed this will take some additional time, which is just fine as I have lots of other details to discuss with you."

Yowza. I already felt sorry for Mrs. Marks, having to have Linney for a daughter and all, but now I feel doubly triply bad for her. Alexandra thumps a giant binder onto the table, and Sadie cringes like she's seen this monstrosity before.

Poor Sades. She's definitely been getting the worst of the wedding-planning stuff since it's her phone we use as our business number, and also because the rest of us kinda figure she knows what she's doing best out of all of us, on account of the years she spent helping her mom. But maybe we should have been more helpful. I'm for sure going to be waaaaay better from now on. I mean, that is if I can take time away from my new favorite hobby—checking my pocket mirror to see what's stuck in my braces *now*.

Alexandra flips to a tab in the middle and flops the book open to a page of photos of women in old-timey dresses. "Okay, girls, now here's what I'm thinking. We send a 'look book' to all of the guests, composed of outfits I would consider appropriate for them to wear in order to match our vintage theme."

Vintage theme? Is this a new one? Because last I knew it was rock-and-roll and before *that* it was fairy tales. I've forgotten the ones that came before those; there've been so very many!

Alexandra doesn't even take a break for air. "For example, here are a slew of early-nineteenth-century fashions that would work well. Perhaps you girls could compile a list of shops in each guest's home city where he or she could procure cloches and elbow-length gloves."

I only know a cloche is a fancy hat because I consider it my duty to be fashion-forward, but I'm guessing Vi has never heard that word. In. Her. Life.

Sadie opens and closes her mouth a few times and then just nods. I gape at her, and when she catches my eye, she gives me a look like *Shh, let me handle this!*, which I am really not so sure about, but I nod too, mostly because she's my bestie and also because one of the little rubber bands in my mouth is doing something distracting and weird.

Next, Alexandra stares at Vi for, like, five whole seconds and then reaches over to touch her ponytail and says, "So, I want to get your take on something, girls. I've asked the blondes in my wedding party to dye their hair brown for the occasion because I want to be the only blonde in my photos. But I'm wondering if I should extend the order to all the guests. You know, in case the photographer wants to get some shots from above. Speaking of which, I think we might need to rent a glider for some aerial shots. I was considering a helicopter, but they're so loud, and since gliders don't have engines . . . or maybe a blimp? Know where we could rent a blimp around here?"

I'm pretty sure my (sore) jaw is on the floor. I steal

a quick glance at Sadie and Vi, and they are studying the linoleum like someone dropped a contact lens. I quickly duck my head down to do the same before I have to be the one to break it to her that the town's only wedding photographer gets so motion sick that just being on a boat makes him barf (exhibit A: the fateful *Little Mermaid* wedding that got Sadie f-i-r-e-d). Which means I'm eleventy-billion percent sure he isn't going up in a blimp. Or a glider. Before any of us can figure out how to yank Alexandra off the cray-cray train, Mrs. Marks appears with a small cake in each hand.

"Who's ready for a sugar buzz?" she sings. We all sigh at the sight of the decorated awesomeness. I'm pretty sure everyone else's are happy sighs. But mine is way more of a *why did I have to ruin my life and get braces so that I'm not even sure if frosting will hurt my teeth?* It *looks* so innocent and squishy, but then again so did the applesauce this morning. Alexandra reaches across the table and grabs a fork out of Mrs. Marks's hand, along with one of the cakes.

"What flavor is this one?"

Mrs. Marks still has her plastered smile. "That's raspberry lemon. This other one here is carrot, and I have my dark chocolate–peanut butter one just about ready."

She sets four plates in front of us and passes me, Sadie, and Vi the other forks.

"It's so nice you girls have this party-planning company. I wish my Linney would find a fun hobby like this."

Writing songs is a hobby. Vi's beach volleyball is a hobby. Sadie's obsessive organizing of school supplies is a . . . well, no, that's just plain weird. But either way, forcing hair dye on unsuspecting wedding guests is not a hobby. It's WORK. Besides, her precious Linney totes has a hobby too. It's called "torturing the rest of us." Sadie just smiles at Mrs. Marks and politely thanks her while Vi mashes her lips together, probably to keep from saying what she really thinks about Linney.

Alexandra is ignoring us and closing her mouth around a forkful of raspberry-lemon cake. She puts it down without comment and reaches across the table to the cake at Sadie's place. She swaps plates and digs into the new one. Eww. She didn't even wipe her fork off or anything. I'm suddenly seeing how this cake tasting is gonna unfold.

Mrs. Marks looks super nervous, probably because Alexandra isn't giving any reaction at all. Like, at *all*. "I'll be right back," Linney's mom says, and disappears into the kitchen again.

By the time she comes back a minute later with the

final cake, Alexandra has taken three more bites of the others, and still: zip zero nada change to her facial expression. She also hasn't offered any to us, so we're just sitting with our forks in our hands looking like we're on a hunger strike or something (which actually might not be that bad of an idea with this whole Great Braces Saga stuff).

Mrs. Marks puts the last cake in front of Alexandra this time, like she knows we're basically not even needed here. Alexandra takes one bite, then puts down her fork. She turns to Sadie and says, "What's the status on those éclairs we talked about? Have you found someone to go to Paris and get them yet?"

Paris?

"Paris?" I ask. I sit way up in my seat because PARIS. Eiffel Tower, Champs-Élysées, most amazing place on Earth (I'm pretty sure).

Sadie kicks me under the table. "I thought we had abandoned that idea, Miss Worthington. I was going to ask our friend Philippe to look into a recipe, remember?

"Philippe?" I ask. I sit *way* up in my seat because PHILIPPE. Floppy hair, adorable accent, most amazing boy on Earth (I'm pretty sure). It sounds like I should have been sitting in on more of these wedding-planning meetings. I'm just saying.

"Right," Alexandra says. "But if we get them, will we have too much chocolate if I go with this last cake?" Before anyone can answer her, she butts in on her own question and answers, "No. That's just silly. There's no such thing as too much chocolate. Maybe we should do a chocolate fountain, too. Write that down, Sadie-babe." She turns to Mrs. Marks and passes her a half-eaten cake. "We'll take the chocolate peanut butter."

Mrs. Marks smiles a huge smile that's totes real this time. "Perfect. This is a crowd-pleaser, I promise. Let me get the order form."

She turns to walk away and Alexandra calls after her, "Oh, and I need it to be nut-free. My fiancé is deathly allergic to peanuts."

Mrs. Marks pauses right in the middle of a step and turns around extra slowly. "Uh, you do realize this is a *peanut*-butter cake. It's made with real peanut butter. I can't see any—"

"Bride's day, bride's way!" Alexandra interrupts. She turns to me. "Am I right, Red? You look like someone who gets her way a lot."

I'm, like, totally incapable of speech (which, if you ask Daddy, never ever happens).

Mrs. Marks resumes trying to explain to Alexandra

how it's not possible to make a nut-free peanut-butter cake, but she is so not having that. Nope. Not one bit.

Alexandra says, "Maybe you could hunt down some nut-free peanut-butter flavoring you could use instead." Then she turns to Sadie and adds, "E-mail my cousin Trent at his lab and ask him to invent something that would work here. And don't let him tell you he can't spare a day away from his infectious-disease study. He can. Tell him the wedding is in just over two weeks, so he needs to get a move on. And keep me updated. I'll get you his e-mail."

With that Alexandra stands up, flips the tail of her long sweater, and flounces out, with a little fluttery hand-wave thing.

Oh. My.

Vi and Sadie are about as tongue-tied as I am, so I do the only thing I can possibly think of. I pull the carrot-cake plate over to me, spin it to find an untouched sliver, then stab it with a fork, and stuff a piece in my mouth.

Owwwwwwwwwwwwwwwwwww.

Vi

12

SUPER-EASY GRANOLA BARS

Ingredients:

1 cup dates (pitted)

1 cup almonds (unsalted, roasted, chopped)

1½ cups rolled oats

¼ cup peanut butter

¼ cup honey

Put the dates into a food processor and chop them for about one minute. Then put them into a bowl with the oats and almonds. Warm the peanut butter and honey in a small pot on the stove (use low heat). Stir the warm peanut butter and honey, and then pour the mixture on top of the oats, almonds, and dates. Mix all the ingredients together (you might have to break up the dates). Put the mixture into an 8" x 8" dish or a small pan (hint: line the dish with parchment paper so the bars don't stick to the bottom). Flatten the mixture by pushing down on it. You want the mixture to be as even-looking as you can get it. Cover the dish with plastic wrap and place it in the refrigerator for at least 15–20 minutes. Once the mixture has hardened, you can remove it from the pan and cut it into approximately 10 bars.

**This is my favorite after-soccer snack!
**They're also really yummy with chocolate chips, raisins, or dried cranberries.

W̶e have problems," Lauren announces the second we're all gathered around the bouquet of flashlights in the *Purple People Eater*.

"Tell me about it," Becca says. "My face hurts and it's freezing in here. I thought my teeth were going to fall out when that wind started blowing outside. So basically I can't open my mouth all winter. Can't we, like, run an extension cord out and plug in a space heater or something?" She shivers and grimaces for extra effect.

"Fire hazard," Lauren replies. "And that's not what I'm talking about."

"Did you get grounded *more*?" I ask. If it were my dad who got a call from the cops in the middle of the night, I'd still be in my room. Heck, he'd probably sit with me in class, which would seriously compound the Linney problem. So basically, while I feel bad for Lauren and Sadie, I'm really glad it wasn't me.

"No! I mean this wedding." Lauren whips out a stack of paper from her backpack. She spreads the pages across the floor and under the glow of the flashlights.

I peer over Sadie's knee at pages and pages of spreadsheets, all printed on this tan-and-pink shell paper. It's So Very Lauren.

Becca recoils from the papers. "What *is* that? It's like math homework gone wild."

"Well, this one shows how much time Sadie's put into this wedding. If you calculate the total time with Sadie's portion of the payment, she's making like, six cents an hour. You know that's breaking approximately ninety labor laws, right?"

"And probably the Geneva Convention." Becca's got this super-serious look on her face. I have no idea what the Geneva Convention is, but from the expression Lauren gives Becca, it has nothing to do with planning Miss Worthington's wedding.

"This one"—Lauren points at a pie chart—"shows how much time we've spent on all aspects of this

wedding. Seventy percent—seventy!—is in the category I call 'Dealing with the Crazy.'"

"She's not crazy," Sadie says.

We all look at her.

"She's just . . . picky. And maybe a little, um . . ."

"Crazy?" I suggest.

"Indecisive," Sadie says.

"She's a total bridezilla." Becca reaches over and
twirls a strand of my hair. I've got it pulled back in
my used-to-be-usual ponytail because I've got a soccer
match later on today. "I mean, she pretty much *ordered*
Vi to dye her hair! Who does that?"

"Crazy people," Lauren answers. "Which is why I
called this meeting. We need to seriously discuss what
to do about this. And, Sades, I know you're not going
to like this, but I think we should bail. She's wasting our
time, and the money isn't worth the hassle."

Sadie's mouth makes a little O.

"Come on, what do y'all think?" Lauren crosses her
arms and waits. "Becca?"

Becca runs her tongue over her braces. "Um . . ."

Lauren shifts her gaze to me. "Vi?"

"Uhhh . . . This is like a come-to-Jesus moment, isn't
it?" That's what Meemaw would call it. As in the truth

comes out and we all have to face it. "In that case, this whole thing with the cluck hats?"

"Cloche," Becca corrects.

"Yeah, those. And the old-fashioned clothes. See, there's this whole group of Ike's family that lives in Wheatfield Corners, Iowa. And I looked it up on the map, and it's not close to anything. At all. So, like, I don't know where they'd go to buy this kind of stuff." Becca was all into looking up these stores for the guests, but the list had gotten so long that I offered to take part of it. I don't know exactly what I was thinking, since hours and hours of looking up weird little stores that sell ancient clothes isn't exactly my idea of a good time.

"They can order online," Sadie says.

"And this thing with the non-nut peanut-butter cake?" Lauren says. "I think that's kind of impossible. Right, Vi?"

"Um . . . probably." I hate feeling like the one who's so down on the wedding. But Lauren's right. It has been every free hour of the day, and whenever we feel like we've gotten something done, Miss Worthington seems to change her mind.

But quitting? I don't really know about that. If we drop Miss Worthington now, these last two months of running around and planning and putting up with her will have been for nothing. Kind of like me dealing with Linney every day at school and never graduating.

And if I'm being honest, I kind of like having something that I can throw myself into to forget about Dad's job and Linney's nasty comments. That thing used to be soccer—until everything got weird with Lance, and Linney made the cheerleading team. Now she's at the games and even a lot of the practices.

"I'm still weirded out by the hair-dyeing thing," Becca says. "And she called me Red. What does that mean, exactly? Is she gonna ask me to change my hair? Because nuh-uh. No way. No how." She runs a hand over her shampoo-commercial-smooth hair. "Although . . . I have been wondering what I'd look like with bangs. . . . Maybe it would distract from the braces. What do y'all think? Bangs? No bangs?" She fans out the ends of her hair across her forehead.

"Bec-*ca*!" Lauren picks up the spreadsheets and taps the edge of the stack so they all line up neatly. "You can talk about your hair later. Right now, we need to decide: Wedding or no wedding? Just think about everything else we could've been doing! Not only could we have booked some parties with normal people and made money by now, but we wouldn't have gotten in trouble. I might not have gotten that B. Becca might have written twenty songs about Philippe—"

"Hey! Who says I want to write about Philippe?" Becca says.

Lauren ignores her. "And, Sadie, things might not be so weird between you and your mom."

"And that's why we can't quit! I mean, not the only reason, but I can't let Mom think we aren't able to handle this. We have to show her that we're just as good at making a wedding happen as she is." Sadie's got her hands flat on the floor on either side of her.

"We have put a lot of work into it already," I add. "And we've only got a couple weeks left, right?"

Lauren turns to Becca. "Don't you want more time to write songs? I *know* I need more hours to study."

"What are you talking about?" Becca asks. "Studying is practically all you've been doing since you got arrested and thrown in the clink by the po-po."

"Becs, we didn't get arrested. It was just a headlight thing," Sadie says before she turns to Lauren. "Even if we were planning other parties, you'd still have to take time away from school stuff. And besides, since when does Lauren Simmons quit *anything*? Did you quit It's

All Academic when Anna got named captain and you didn't?"

"Well, no. But that's not the same—"

"What about when that summer weekly came in and demanded a tour of the marina for, like, a whole day and then didn't even end up docking his fancy-pants yacht here after all?" Becca says. "You didn't tell your dad that you weren't going to work there anymore."

"Wait, I thought you were on my side. You *like* working for Miss Worthington?" Lauren asks Becca. "What about the hair-dye thing?"

Becca waves her hand. "She can talk all she wants. None of us are changing our hair for her. What I know is that we'll be washing our hands of her in two weeks. After she pays us, good riddance."

"No quitting now, Lauren." I jump in. I can't stand Miss Worthington either, but no way did I just spend hours and hours researching silly hats for nothing. And if I had all that free time back, I'd probably be thinking too much. About Lance. About Linney. About the dance. About Lance-and-Linney. About Linney hanging on Lance like a shadow ever since the dance. And about Dad, who hasn't mentioned that I asked him to quit his job, even though it's been two weeks. He's just been acting normal, which means he's not going to change his mind and quit. I feel like I should understand that, especially after Lauren brought up the possibility of us quitting the wedding. But I've tried, and I still don't understand it. Even though it's nice to have him around more, I'm miserable at the same time.

"We're in this till the end." I put my hand over the flashlights, palm down.

Sadie and Becca stack their hands on top of mine.

"Come on, Lo," Becca says.

"Tough it out," I add. Like I'm toughing out my school/Dad situation.

Slowly, as she rolls her eyes, Lauren drops her hand on top of Sadie's. "Fine. But I have to devote at least three hours per night to school, okay? I don't care if Miss Worthington is floating out to sea with those six hundred paper lanterns she was dead set on last week and I'm the only one who can throw her a life vest. I *can't* get another B."

"RSVP!" I shout.

"RSVP!" they echo.

"We just have to set limits, that's all," Sadie says as she stands up. "Somehow."

"I think she's stuck with us, no matter what." Becca

hands the bucket of flashlights to Lauren. "It's too late for her to find another wedding planner now."

"Okay, so the next time she makes some outrageous demand, we have to talk her out of it. Right?" I wrap my arms around myself as Lauren clicks off all the flashlights and stows them on the *PPE*'s countertop. Becca's right. It is freezing in here. I guess that means fall has finally arrived in Sandpiper Beach.

"Right," Lauren says. She leads the way up the narrow stairs. "No more running when she calls. Okay, Sadie?"

"Well, I mean, if it's not a big deal, and I'm not doing anything anyway, I don't mind, really."

"Sadie!" Becca stands on deck with her hands on her hips. "The whole point of this going-to-church—"

"Come-to-Jesus," I correct her.

"Yeah, that. The whole point was to make it clear that things have to change! And it has to be all of us making the change. Including you."

Sadie hops off the *PPE* onto the dock. "Okay, I promise."

"All for one, and one for all, y'all," Becca says with a big grin. The second she smiles, the wind gusts. "Oww."

VI

The sun has warmed everything up and the wind's died down by the time the game against the Live Oak Beach Coquinas starts. Our Pirate Pelican mascot is dancing along the sidelines. I always thought he was one of the worst mascots in the history of team mascots—until I saw the Coquina. At least the Pirate Pelican can look a little fierce. The Coquina just sort of . . . stands there. Because it's basically a clam in a shell, it doesn't really have legs or arms or anything. At the bare minimum, they should have stuck an eye patch around its shell. At least the Coquina is so big that it hides the one person I really don't want to see—Linney. But I know she's back there, probably moving a single strand of honey-gold-highlighted hair back into place and glaring at everyone.

As I take my position on the field, I scan the bleachers for familiar faces. There, right in the very front, are Lauren, Sadie, and Becca. And Dad. I wave at them, giving myself a second to enjoy the fact that Dad is here to watch me, and then I get my head into the game. We win the coin toss and give the Coquinas the kickoff to start.

I move through the actions, focusing on the ball and the strategy. At one point in the first half, I've got the ball. I keep it close, moving straight toward the goal.

I have one focus, and that's to make that ball connect with net. Nothing else matters.

Even though I'm zeroed in on where I'm going, I'm still completely aware of the guy next to me in his purple Coquinas uniform. I maneuver this way and that to keep him away from the ball. But just as I get into kicking distance to the goal, he leaps in front of me and steals the ball away. I kick out to get it back and completely wipe out, landing smack on my back as he moves away with the ball.

"You okay?" Lance reaches out a hand. This summer, he would've cracked some joke about me tripping over my own feet. And then I would've said something really smart-alecky back. But now he just asks if I'm okay.

I kinda miss the old Lance.

"Yeah, just give me a second." I lie there on the grass, trying to catch my breath as the referee blows his whistle for play to stop. I roll my head to the right, just in time to see Dad stand up, looking really concerned. My friends stand too—until Sadie pulls her phone from her purse. Then she sits down. It's probably Miss Worthington, asking if we can relocate the entire wedding to Outer Mongolia or someplace.

One of the referees comes jogging over to me. I'd better get up before they think I'm really hurt.

"Let me help you," Lance says, sticking his hand out again.

"I'm fine. I don't need any help." I dig my palms into the grass and push myself up. I know he's my teammate and is supposed to show concern and all, but I'm not falling for it. Especially since he's already turned away from me and is looking right at Linney in her Pirate Pelicans cheerleading outfit. She's leading some kind of chant, out in front with the other girls behind her.

I don't really care what Linney's doing or not doing, so I nod to the referee to show him I'm okay. I'm just about to wave to Coach Robbins when I hear it.

"Kick that ball! Don't fall!"

No way is Linney directing that cheer at me. She couldn't do that, not here, in front of everyone.

"Hey, *boys!*" she shouts, looking directly at me.

"Hey, what?" the other cheerleaders yell back.

"Kick that ball! Don't fall!"

I'm pretty sure my cheeks are going pink. Lance is still watching her. I can't see what he's doing, but he's making some kind of motion with his hands. Probably clapping or something.

I really can't believe that I ever liked him like that, even a little.

The referee blows his whistle again, and the game swings back into action. I'm so focused on playing that I don't hear anything beyond the shouts of my teammates until halftime.

I follow everyone over to the sidelines and grab a bottle of water. Up in the stands, Dad gives me a huge smile. I grin back. Even though no one's scored yet, it's still been a good game. It's nice to have him here, even if it means I have to see him in that navy-blue uniform tomorrow, sweeping the stairs at school.

Next to him, Lauren and Becca wave. Sadie's not there—she must've had to go to the bathroom or something. Since we agreed not to jump when Miss Worthington called, I know she couldn't have run off to do anything wedding related. My heart fills up when I realize that everyone I love the most is here, just to see me.

I'm leaning against the fence, talking strategy with Katie Asselin and the twins Ben and Jack Molanari, when the cheerleaders take the field. I have all the respect in the world for the girls who do crazy flips and stunts that I'd probably break my neck trying, but

Linney is the *last* person I want to see. Especially when I've got half a game left to play.

Ben's showing Jack, Katie, and me how to do a Cruyff turn (using his fingers as legs) when the cheerleaders burst into another cheer.

"Two, four, six, eight! Who do we appreciate?" they all shout in unison.

"Lance, Lance, goooooo, Lance!" And *that* would be Linney.

From over by the water bottles, Lance's face goes beet red. I smirk—just a little. Totally serves him right.

"Vi, what do you think?" Ben asks.

"Oh, um, that's good," I say, even though I wasn't paying attention to him at all. Which is So Not Vi. Why I am more concerned with Linney than I am with the game?

I try really hard to listen to Ben, Jack, and Katie debate more strategy, but I keep getting distracted. After embarrassing a bunch of other guys and girls on the team, the cheerleaders move on to something about . . . violets?

I slowly turn my head until I can see Linney leaping around in the middle of the field.

"Why have a violet when you can have a rose?

Cheer for the Pelicans from your head to your toes!"
Linney shouts. Then she jumps up and touches her toes.
Because obviously. "Roses are so pretty, and they always
win. Violets are the last pick, and they stick like a pin.
Cheer for the Pelicans to score a ten!"

I can't believe it. She totally made that cheer up.
Besides being really bad and not making any sense, it's
so clearly about me. I'm the violet and she's, what, the
rose? It almost makes me want to laugh, except I wonder if anyone else has gotten it.

Lance looks right at me. He gets it. He frowns and
shakes his head.

Please. I don't need his pity. Being pitiful is So Not
Vi. I look back up into the stands, at the people who
really matter. Dad's watching Linney too, and he doesn't
look all that happy. Maybe this is good. . . . After seeing
how awful Linney's being, in front of everyone from
parents to the team from Live Oak Beach, maybe he'll
finally get how hard his job is making school for me.
And maybe he'll quit.

That itty-bitty glimmer of hope makes me just a
tiny bit happy—for a second. Then I remember that if
Dad didn't have this school job, he wouldn't be here at
my game. And we wouldn't get to take the kayaks out as

much as we can now, and I'd go back to eating a lot of dinners by myself.

Linney repeats the whole entire awful violets/roses cheer. I'm not so sure now that I want Dad to go back to construction. Having him here—with me—is one of the best things ever. I love that he's sitting there, with my friends. Except, wait . . . I look to Dad's left again, where Sadie, Becca, and Lauren should be.

They aren't there.

Even as halftime ends (complete with Linney shouting, "Don't fall again, okay, Violet?" as she runs off the field), my friends still aren't in their seats. As I move into position with my team, I finally remember why.

Alexandra Worthington. Who insisted that today was the only day she could get to the church to plan every millisecond of the wedding ceremony, from how many seconds need to be between each bridesmaid's walk down the aisle to testing how far the musicians will have to sit from the guests so the music will be the perfect volume.

I hate that my friends aren't here to see the end of the game, but at least Dad is. And so I ignore Linney's smug face, try to bury my annoyance at Alexandra Worthington, and just concentrate on playing for Dad.

I don't think about Lance at all. Not one little bit.

Sadie

13

TODAY'S TO-DO LIST:

- ☐ confirm dress pickup
- ☐ make candles in vintage teacups
- ☐ finish tying labels on key wedding favors
- ☐ fold old-fashioned paper fans out of the printed wedding programs
- ☐ call caterer and check on whether their forks have three tongs or four, and report back to AW
- ☐ e-mail directions to hotel to AW's third cousin
- ☐ see how much Zach will charge to drive us to the mall in Wilmington to pick out bridesmaid gifts for twelve
- ☐ get Vi to bake Zach some s'mores bars to bribe Zach if money alone won't do it

- ☐ talk Lauren into stealing Zach's game controller if food and money aren't enough
- ☐ finish math homework
- ☐ find binders to organize all wedding documents/contracts in—one copy for each member of RSVP
- ☐ put all papers in binders, color code red for Becca, yellow for Lauren, green for Vi, and blue for me
- ☐ EVERYTHING ELSE (AND THERE'S SO SO SO MUCH!)

Izzy, you are the absolute *best* sibling anywhere. Seriously. I mean it."

My little sister goes all pink. "You're just saying that because I'm helping you tie tags around all these old-timey keys." She threads a piece of brown twine through the hole in the top of one, slips on a tag that says LOVE IS THE KEY TO EVERYTHING, and ties them off.

"Maybe. But you have to admit, these are awesome, right?" I'm super proud of myself for coming up with this idea for wedding favors. Way better than the dolphin bobbleheads we returned. They're perfect for the vintage theme, and best of all, Alexandra Worthington loves the idea. Which means I love it doubly much.

Izzy shrugs. "If you're into this kind of thing."

"Yeah, well, maybe I am." I only have twenty-seven pages of Pinterest ideas on my Alexandra Worthington Vintage Wedding board, so I'd say, yeah, maybe.

Izzy picks up another key and begins the process over again. "How come the other girls aren't here doing this with you?"

I jostle my shoulder into hers. "You're the one who was complaining I didn't spend enough time with you. I thought you might find this fun. Besides, you said you wanted to help, remember?"

Izzy nods and adds another finished one to the pile. "I'm not complaining. Geez. I was just asking."

The truth is I really did want to spent time with Izzy, because I'm trying hard to be the big sister I promised Dad I would be and also because I sort of, kind of, even like hanging out with Iz sometimes. But the rest of the truth is that I was a little bit afraid to invite the other girls to help. I don't want them to have so much to do that they reconsider their vote to keep going with the wedding planning. No one was happy when we could only stay for part of Vi's soccer game before we had to meet Miss Worthington at the church. Now we're only two days away from the big day, and they each have lists of their own to work on. Becca's already in charge of putting together a playlist for the bands (note the plural *s* on that), Vi has to round up some of her teammates from soccer to help us hang these cool mason jars wrapped in lace doilies at the ceremony site, and Lauren is crunching numbers on the budget big-time. Everyone has something to do. So what if I have a few extra somethings?

I can handle it.

Plus I have Izzy to help me.

"How was school, my sweet girls? Whatcha up to?" Mom comes in, tugging the ends of her hair through a ponytail holder. Her flip-flops *thunk* across the floor as she approaches.

"I'm helping!" Izzy proclaims, and I hide a smile at how proud she sounds. Bonus big-sister points to me.

"I can see that!" Mom smoothes the top of Izzy's hair down and squeezes her shoulders. "Is this for the wedding? Too cute, Sadie!"

For what seemed like forever it felt really super tense around Mom whenever anything wedding-related came up, and if this were last month, I probably would have found somewhere else to do this so I could avoid all mention of the Event That Shall Not Be Named, but lately she's been bringing it up more and more in casual ways like this, and it hasn't been so bad.

"Yeah. These are the favors. The wedding's a vintage theme so . . ."

"They're perfect!" Mom picks one up and examines it from every angle. "Completely perfect. I may have to steal this idea someday."

My insides get as warm and gooey as a roasted marshmallow, and I can't hide my smile. Mom smiles back, then says, "Hey, so if you're ready for a break, I'm planning to take advantage of the nice weather we've been having the last couple days to hit the surf for some pre-dinner boogie boarding."

I'm not sure whose eyebrows are higher—Izzy's or mine. "Boogie boarding? You?"

Mom just grins. "Well, yeah. There's some storm in the Caribbean that's sending great waves our way. I thought it might be fun. But fun is way *more* fun when it's with my two favorite girls. Whaddya say?"

Izzy is already halfway up the stairs *and* halfway out of her jeans. "I'm coming! Just gotta grab my wet suit!"

Mom laughs and turns to me. "Sades. C'mon. A

break would do you good. Don't think I haven't noticed how hard you've been working on this wedding."

I look down at the mess of keys waiting for tags and catch sight of my to-do list on the chair next to me. It's only got two small lines crossed through a verrrrrrry long number of items.

"Better not. Duty calls." I motion to the tabletop and shrug. If anyone should get that, it would be Mom. She's always missing out to do stuff for her clients.

Mom looks like she's about to talk me out of staying, but then she just says, "Well, if you change your mind, we'll be in the cove. I don't know what the undertow is like near the pier, so we'll stick close to home."

I nod and go back to stringing a label. A few minutes later the house is so quiet I can hear the laundry upstairs tumbling around the dryer. I set a rhythm that matches the *thump-thump* as I thread and tie, thread and tie, but when the dryer buzzes, I decide the quiet is too much and flip on the TV in the kitchen. It's some stupid talk show, but I don't care. It keeps me company while I work.

I finish the favors and pack them safely into a box before setting up the candle-making supplies I got from Party Me Hearties. The plan is to melt wax into these really cute mismatched vintage teacups Becca found at the antiques store above Polka Dot Books. There'll be a few for every table, and I think they're going to look fantastic. I just have no idea how long it will take to get them that way. This would be way more fun if I had someone to make them with.

I pick up my phone to text Lauren, not to see if she can come over (even though her grounding is done, she's sticking hard to her own no-going-out-on-school-nights rule) but just to have someone to talk to. We've been texting back and forth because her vocab word this week is "irony" and even she can't explain what the heck "a situation in which actions have an effect that is opposite from what was intended, so that the outcome is contrary to what was expected" means. She keeps saying, "I just know it when I see it." So all day long I've been texting her my guesses. I scroll through this morning's:

Getting the flu on UR vacation?

Nope. That's just bad luck.

Winning lottery & then dying next day?

Also bad luck. But if you died by excessive paper cuts from giant check the lottery commission gave you, *that* would be ironic.

I still don't totally get it. But this time I think I just might have a decent guess:

Starting party planning company to get ur Mom to hire u back so u could spend time 2gether, then not being able to spend time w/her bc ur too busy w/stuff 4 company?

Her text back comes almost immediately.

Um, yeah. That would be irony. Also: *hugs*

That's what I thought. I drop my phone into my pocket and get back to business. I'm nearly done with the candles when Mom and Izzy push through the door, dripping water from their ponytails and jumping up and down with their arms behind their backs trying to get their wet suits unzipped and peeled off.

"Sadie, you should have seen the waves. They were, like, monsters!" Izzy's pupils are so wide I can barely see the hazel parts.

"It was a little intense," Mom adds. "And the water was weirdly warm. Oh, and we saw two seals, right, Iz?"

"Yup. And Mom says maybe we can go back out tomorrow! Right, Mom?"

Mom motions for Izzy to step onto a towel she's laid out on the floor and uses a second one to mop the wet spots from the floor. "Maybe, Iz. Depends on what those waves are doing. That storm is moving north. Last I heard it was headed for the Bahamas later this week, and that'll make the waves even bigger, so . . . oh! The weather is on now—Sades, turn it up a little, please."

I hadn't even noticed that the talk show had turned into the news. I guess I got more into candle making than I realized. I reach for the remote and punch up the volume.

"*. . . repeat that we're now seeing a change in the trajectory of this storm. While our models here show it turning out to sea, new storm models out of Europe project a path for coastal North Carolina, with landfall predicted for Friday evening around nine p.m. With water temperatures warmer than usual for this time of year, the storm is expected to pick up traction as it makes its way up the coast and may come ashore as a Category One hurricane, with sustained winds of eighty-five miles per hour. Tropical Storm Susannah is one we'll be keeping a very close eye on here in the weather center, folks. Stay tuned for more updates as Storm Watch Susannah continues.*"

Without realizing I'm doing it, I uncurl my fingers, and the teacup I'm holding nearly slips out of my hand. "But . . . but . . . that's tomorrow. And the wedding is on Saturday. We can't have a *hurricane* the night before the wedding!"

"We'll figure it out, Sadie. Don't worry," Mom says, taking the teacup out of my hand and setting it gently on the counter.

"Don't worry? Don't worry! How am I supposed to not worry when the most important event ever that I've spent every spare second getting ready for might have to happen in six-hundred-mile-per-hour winds? The glider for the overhead pictures won't even be able to take off, and I doubt the photographer from Nags Head we found to do it would even try to get here! This is—it's just—I don't even know."

I sink into a chair, and Mom sits down next to me and takes my hand. Izzy plops down on the other side of my mother and tucks herself under Mom's arm. "Glider for overhead . . . ?" Mom starts, then says, "Never mind. Something tells me I don't even want to know. Hey. I get it. I do. I once had a wedding ceremony take place in the same church where a funeral for a firefighter was happening in the next chapel. You couldn't even hear the bride say "I do" over all the sirens outside honoring him. But, honey, even you can't control the weather."

"But, *Moooooom.* Alexandra Worthington is not going to accept that as an excuse. She'll probably want me to hunt down some voodoo doctor to reverse the storm direction or something."

I can tell Mom is trying not to smile (even though I could totally see Alexandra asking for that). "Well, then you'll just have to tell her to take it up with your mother. Because if this storm is headed our way, we're not going to be worried about a wedding, that's for sure. I'm sure you've heard me and Dad talk about Hurricane Floyd. It happened before you and Iz were born, but it killed fifty-seven people and caused billions in damage from all the flooding. Granted, that was a much stronger hurricane and conditions were different, but still. These storms are nothing to mess around with. My first and only priority is keeping our family safe. And I want staying safe to be the only thing you're focused on too."

I burst into tears. Mostly about the wedding stuff, but maybe a little bit from fear, too, because hurricanes are super scary and even though we all live with the threat of them because of where Sandpiper Beach is on the coast, I haven't ever been here for one. Usually we get enough warning that Mom has us in the car and driving to my grandparents' in West Virginia before it even gets windy. That thought stops my tears.

"We're not going to Grandma's, are we?" I ask. My

heart is pounding. I absolutely, positively cannot cross state lines with the wedding so close.

Mom frowns a little and wipes the leftover tear streaks from my face. "I don't think we have time if they're talking about tomorrow night. I have to board up the windows and do all the rest of the storm prep. Hopefully, the projections are off and it turns out to sea, but I think we'll be riding this one out at the shelter."

Izzy whimpers and Mom turns to comfort her. "Don't worry, Izzy-fizz. It will be like a giant Sandpiper Beach sleepover."

"Will my friends be there?" Izzy asks.

"You bet!" says Mom, tugging Iz's ponytail.

Izzy jumps up and races up the stairs. "I have to call Morgan and tell her!"

Mom watches her go with a small smile, then turns back to me. "So listen. I know we haven't really talked much about this wedding stuff, and I want you to know how proud of you I am. From everything I can see, you're doing an amazing job, and I know from the time I spent with her that Alexandra is not the easiest of clients."

I can't help a snort at that understatement, but I hide it in my sleeve because I really, really want to hear the rest of what Mom has to say about how awesome I am. Compliments from Mom are always the best, but compliments from Mom about *wedding planning* are the best of the best. I mean, really, they're kind of my dream come true after everything that went down with the firing. But I totally don't expect the next words out of her mouth.

"However, Sades, I want you to ease up a little."

"What?!"

"I know, I know. Maybe this is the pot calling the kettle black. But I've had a lot of time to think about this stuff these last few months. I'm sure you've noticed I've been less busy."

I hang my head. If I hadn't gotten Mom fired, she would be plenty busy. It's all my fault she's had plenty of time on her hands. "I know. I'm so, so sorry, Mom. I didn't know you were her wedding planner when she first called us, and then Becca told her—"

"Hey. Hey!" Mom uses her finger to lift my chin up so that I'm looking at her. "Is that what you think? That I haven't been busy because you took my client away?"

I nod, trying to form words over the giant lump in my throat. "And then you were talking about how I shouldn't get too many clothes for school 'cause money was tight and . . ." I have to stop talking because I start crying too hard.

Mom tugs me in tight to her chest. Her skin smells like salt water and her towel like dryer sheets. Mostly she smells like Mom. Safe.

"Sades, really? You thought that was your fault? I have brides calling every day. I could do twice the number of weddings if I wanted to, but I realized this summer how much I was missing. I felt awful not being there on Illumination Night when Izzy got sick, and when I saw how much you were doing with RSVP, it made me realize how grown-up you were getting. I didn't want to miss that anymore, so I met with my financial advisor and we figured out a way I could scale back the business to be home more. Sure, we have to watch our spending, but we're just fine. *I'm* just fine. I had no idea you thought I was upset or that you thought you caused anything bad to happen."

She pulls her fingers through my hair and sighs. "Baby, we have *got* to get better at communicating. *Especially* with your teenage years ahead." She tucks a stray piece behind my ear. "Can we make a vow to talk more openly with each other?"

I nod and swipe a few stray tears off my cheek. All

this time I thought Mom was so sad about the wedding stuff. Or mad. I don't really know. I guess I've been so focused on the wedding that even though I noticed Mom has been around a whole lot more, I didn't really want to acknowledge it or think about it because I felt so guilty it was all because of me. I'm such an idiot.

Mom takes my hand and squeezes it. "Listen. I want you to hear me when I say this. Dialing back on work stuff has made me realize something. There are more important things in life than a wedding that happens on just one day out of a whole lifetime of days. Celebrations are wonderful and very special ways to mark occasions, but *real life* is everything that goes on between those big events. That's where the *most* important stuff happens. Does that make sense?"

Not totally, but I guess I get what she's saying. I might need to think about it more later, like when I'm trying to fall asleep tonight. For now I squeeze Mom's hand back. "So, um, you'll be around more, like, for good?"

"Hopefully. Or at least for as long as I can make it work," Mom says with a smile. She wraps an arm around my shoulder and holds me close until Izzy clomps back downstairs to inform us she's made a list of snack foods she wants to bring to "the town sleepover."

Mom tugs Izzy over the back of the couch so she lands on top of us, then tickles her. "A list, huh? I don't know, Sades. I think we might have yet another party planner in the Pleffer family."

The giggles from all three of us drown out the light wind that's starting to blow outside.

Sandpiper Beach Hurricane Evacuation Manual, page 3

The following are suggested items to bring
with you to a storm shelter. Please bring only
essentials and limit your belongings to:

- personal toiletries
- pillows, blankets, and other bedding
(cots will be provided)
- nonperishable food items to snack on
- change of clothes
- baby supplies, if applicable
- medications
- cash
- battery-operated radio and flashlight
- important documents such as birth or marriage
certificates, insurance policies, and social security cards
- board games, cards, or other forms of entertainment

14

Lauren

angst noun \ ˈäŋ(k)st, ˈaŋ(k)st \
a feeling of being worried or nervous; anxiety about
a situation
Use in a sentence:
This hurricane is causing RSVP—and Alexandra
Worthington—a lot of angst.

$\mathcal{S}$andpiper Beach Middle School looks just like those
places you see on TV that have been turned into shelters from natural disasters. Cots marching in lines down
the gym, volunteers running around all over, and tables
set up everywhere with people playing cards, talking on
their phones, or doing work on tablets and laptops.

Except it's not on TV. It's real.

I'd say it's no big deal, but honestly . . . I'm a little
scared. Instead of waking up to go to school for English

and science this morning, I woke up to go to school with my mom, bags of our stuff, and the entire population of the island. (Which is only 4,042 people, but when everyone's stuffed into SBMS, it looks more like the population of New York City.) Plus, it's weird to see the gym—a place I normally avoid like the plague because I have a genuine fear of basketballs and volleyballs and pretty much anything that requires me to be the least bit coordinated—turned into a giant motel. Usually we have enough warning that Mom takes me and my brothers to our aunt Leticia's in High Point, while Dad sticks around for marina emergencies. But not this time. This storm came up so *fast*.

"When will Dad and Zach get here?" I ask Mom as she's surveying the cots. They went out at first light to finish nailing boards on the windows of the marina office and to help customers prepare their boats to survive the storm.

"Soon, honey, I promise. Your dad's been through this before, and he won't stay out longer than it's safe." She squeezes my hand, and then points to five free cots in the very back. "How about there?"

I nod, and we go dump our stuff on the beds. Even though I'll probably end up moving my cot closer to my friends.

"What about Bubby?" I ask as I unpack my phone charger, my science book, a notebook, and some blank index cards. "We should've gone to pick her up."

"I called earlier, and the senior center is bringing everyone here on buses. They'll be here soon. Are you studying?" Mom looks at me as if it's completely unheard of to make flash cards for your upcoming science test in a hurricane shelter.

"Of course."

She shakes her head, but I can tell she's smiling just a little. My heart soars. After the whole golf cart/police incident, I've been working overtime to get my grades back to normal and to prove to my parents that I'm still the same old Lauren. I was just sidetracked, is all, and now I'm 100 percent dedicated to my future. Unlike Zach, who just got his ACT score back. It's actually not bad—he could've gotten into Raleigh State like Josh if he bothered to have decent grades. But when your GPA is something like 1.5, it's kind of hard to convince colleges to take a chance on you.

Mom drifts off to watch the meteorologists on the TV set up in the corner. I've managed to tune out the constant chatter and babies crying and occasional laughter and actually have a good stack of flash cards going when Becca's face pops up in front of my notes.

"Lauren! What are you doing, crazypants? Who studies when there's a *hurricane* outside?" Her braces gleam in the fluorescent lights of the gym.

"There's no hurricane yet, just some wind," I inform her as I gently push her head away so I can see my notes again.

"We're going to see what's for lunch," Sadie says from behind Becca.

Vi makes a face. "Do you think it's the same food we get for school lunch? Last time I was here, it was." Both Vi and Becca have done the school-shelter thing before, but it's been a couple of years since the last time we had a hurricane headed this way.

"I bet it's something better this time. Like those turkey-and-pear sandwiches from Pipin' Hot Cafe. And cupcakes from Marks'." Becca's smile disappears as she runs a tongue over her teeth.

"I can't believe they still hurt." I feel kind of bad for Becca. And at the same time very thankful that I inherited already-straight teeth from my mom.

"A little, but they're getting better," she says. "Hey, maybe there's soup!"

"Okay. Let me just finish this card." I scratch out the last few words in a definition of *osmosis*. Then I tuck the flash cards into my pocket.

"Oh no. No, no, no. You're not bringing that to lunch." Becca tries to pull the cards out of my pocket, but I swat her hand away.

"Let her bring them," Sadie says. "But at lunch we have to discuss a backup plan for the wedding."

At the mention of the word "wedding," my stomach gets all tangled up. Because, honestly, I don't see how it's going to happen if we're all stuck here. I mean, the rehearsal was supposed to be at six o'clock tonight— three hours before the hurricane is predicted to make landfall. I don't think we're going to be rehearsing much of anything tonight, except maybe how to study when the power goes out.

"Do you think there will . . . ," Vi starts to say as we make our way through the cots and people toward the gym door. She glances at Sadie as if she's almost afraid to say any more. "I mean, can it happen tomorrow? If we're all here and there's a hurricane coming overnight?"

We pass the knot of people standing around the TV and stop as a unit when we hear the newscast. "The storm has reached sustained winds of seventy-five miles per hour and is now a Category One hurricane. The National Weather Service has declared a hurricane warning for the coasts of North and South Carolina. Don't fool around with this storm, people. Get to a shelter immediately. Hurricane Susannah is due to make landfall somewhere in the Wilmington area around nine o'clock this evening. . . ."

Sadie's biting her lip, and I can tell she's trying hard not to cry. All this work, putting up with Miss Worthington, and it might be for nothing. I wrap an arm around her shoulders and squeeze. She gives me a tentative smile.

"It'll be okay," she says in a wobbly voice.

"Abso-posi-lutely," Becca adds. "RSVP doesn't give up that easily. We've taken on Linney Marks and her devious fashion show plans *and* a mob of boy-crazy eight-year-old girls. We'll figure something out."

I catch Mom's eye and point to the door. She nods and goes back to watching the news.

"Come on," I say decisively. "Let's get some food, and then maybe we can come up with a contingency plan."

"A what?" Vi asks as she pushes open the door.

"Contingency. A provision for an unforeseen event."

"Huh?" Becca says.

"Never mind. A backup plan." We head down the hall from the gym in the middle of the school toward the lobby and the main entrance. The entryway is full of tables set up with volunteers—including Vi's dad, who organized the whole thing—to check people in. I hate to think of *why* the town wants to check people in. I mean, the only reason for keeping track of who shows up here is to account for missing people if the hurricane wipes out Sandpiper Beach. Which pulls up images of my house filling with water—all of Dad's boat knickknacks and my It's All Academic and spelling-bee trophies and Mom's china floating around inside. Our house is one of the oldest ones on the island, which means it was built without pilings. It just sits flat on the ground like a normal inland house, waiting to get flooded. Or worse, the wind blows so hard the house just disintegrates, and we have nothing left. Everything we have, gone. Just like that.

"Lauren?" Vi asks. "Are you okay?"

I swallow. "Yeah. It's just a little scary, you know. This hurricane."

She nods. "I know. Meemaw's house is right on the beach." Front row, meaning front lines for the hurricane.

I glance at my friends, who all look a little freaked out. Sadie's house is just across from the cove at the end of the island, and Becca's is right smack in the middle, not too far from the square.

Becca gives a nervous laugh. "Let's go eat and talk about Lauren's convict plan."

"Contingency," I correct her.

"Whatever. I'm starving." She leads the way out of the lobby, with its giant Pirate Pelican looking down on us all, into the cafeteria.

I bring up the rear, after standing on my tiptoes to peek out the front doors' windows. It looks the same outside as it did when Mom and I got here. Windy, no rain.

In the cafeteria, we collect food (lasagna, which is exactly what was on the menu for school lunch today) and gather at our usual table near the wall. It's weird seeing so many adults and little kids here. Even Ms. Snyder, my math teacher, is sitting near the door with her husband and three children. I wave at Anna Wright and some other people from It's All Academic.

"If I'd known this was going to be regular old school lunch," Vi says as she picks at her lasagna, "I would've packed something like I usually do. I have some leftover tortellini and Alfredo sauce in the fridge at home that's calling my name right now."

Becca's chewing very, very carefully, and Sadie just pushes her food around on her plate.

"Has anyone seen Miss Worthington?" I ask. I almost expect her to appear out of nowhere, demanding that we set up a wedding right here in the school cafeteria, complete with exotic flowers from Central American rain forests and neon lighting straight from Vegas.

"Not yet," Sadie says.

"When she gets here, I think we need to hide," Vi says. "The sports-equipment closet is big enough for us all."

I kind of want to agree with Vi. Who wants to be stuck in a confined space with Alexandra Worthington breathing down our necks constantly?

"That's crazy," Becca says.

"No, *she's* crazy," Vi replies. "There are mats in there we could sleep on. Think of how peaceful it would be. Plus, we wouldn't have to hear Linney."

Linney's voice is echoing above all the other chatter in the cafeteria, complaining about how her mother wouldn't let her take more than one suitcase full of stuff to the shelter, and she had to leave behind her hair dryer and the dress she'd already bought for the winter mixer in December. And she's saying all this to Lance, who's stuck holding both his tray of food and hers. He looks like he'd rather be anywhere than here. Like, even facing down a hurricane on the pier right now.

Vi rolls her eyes.

"So, ideas, anyone?" I say, trying to distract Vi. "About the wedding, I mean? Just in case we can't have it this weekend."

We throw around a few thoughts, most of which I'm pretty sure Miss Worthington will hate and which will take weeks to put together. And that means weeks more of dealing with Miss Worthington, when we all thought our nightmare with her would be over after tomorrow.

We're just finishing up when Sadie's phone beeps. She looks at it, and then holds it out so we can all read the text.

Sadie-babe, Ikey and I are going to ride out this storm at his house. Come by in 15 and bring those favors. I want to make sure you used the dusky pink teacups instead of the rose pink.

"I'm sorry, what?" I blink at that text as if the words are going to change.

"She's lost it," Vi says.

"Don't answer her," Becca says.

"We *have* to say something." Sadie's turned her phone back around and is staring at the screen.

"Tell her that if she has even a shred of sense, she'll get her butt down here now." I push my tray aside and hold out my hand. "I'll tell her."

"No," Sadie says. "We're not making her mad."

"It's saving her life. I don't care if she's mad."

"Fine, I'll suggest it to her. Nicely." Sadie's quiet while she types. "Okay, how's this? '*We are at the middle-school shelter and not allowed to leave. Please come here. It's not safe on the beach.*'"

"I think you should add 'you cray-cray' to the end of that," Becca advises.

"Um, no." Sadie hits send.

"Hey, is that your dad?" Vi points somewhere past my shoulder.

I turn and spot Dad and Zach making their way through the crowd to the line for lunch. I jump up and race toward them, barreling into Dad, who's soaking wet. I guess it's started raining.

"You're here!" I say, my voice muffled by his Sandpiper Beach Marina polo shirt.

"Of course we're here," he says, running a hand down my hair as I squeeze the breath out of him.

"Oof," Zach says when I let go of Dad and launch myself at my brother.

"I was worried about you," I say when I finally let go.

"You didn't need to worry," Dad says. "We're all here and safe now."

"Except Bubby," I tell her. "Sandpiper Active Senior Living was supposed to send everyone in on buses."

"They'll be here soon, I'm sure," Dad says, but his smile is pinched at the corners.

"Miss Worthington just texted back," Vi informs me when I return to our table. "She doesn't understand why we can't leave the shelter and come to Ike's."

"And she's not coming here. Totes cray-cray, I told you," Becca adds. She passes me a pretty white-and-yellow-frosted cupcake. "Here, Mrs. Marks came by handing these out. Something about how they were for a birthday party today and she didn't want them to go to waste." Becca looks at the cupcake with sad eyes. "They make my teeth hurt."

I peel the wrapper away and polish off the cupcake in a few bites. I figure it's best to get rid of it so Becca doesn't have to look at it longer than necessary. Plus, it's really good.

"So, what did you say to Miss Worthington?" I ask Sadie after I swallow the last bite of cupcakey goodness.

She frowns. "Pretty much the same thing I said before. Then I told her my mom was making me turn off my phone to save the battery in case the power goes out. I feel bad lying to her."

"Way better than, like, putting up with all her loconess all night," Becca says.

I agree with Becca, but right now I'm actually worried about Miss Worthington and Ike fending off the hurricane in his beach house. It's front row, too, like Vi's house. "Do you think we should tell someone?" I ask my friends. "Like the police? Just so they know they're out there in case . . ." I can't finish the sentence.

Sadie nods. "Let's go find an officer."

"I think I saw Officer Davis at the door," Vi says. "He was telling people they can't bring in their pets." She chews on her lip, and I know she's thinking of her cat, Buster, at the animal shelter up in Wilmington.

"He's gonna be fine," Becca says. "He knows he's coming back home. Cats are smart like that, you know?"

Vi gives her a slight smile as we all get up to deposit

our trays and go back to the lobby. When we get there, Sadie spots Officer Davis at the door with Becca's parents, talking to newcomers carrying in suitcases and bags of stuff. We push our way through the people to reach him.

Just as Sadie is telling him about Miss Worthington, a few volunteers, including Vi's dad and Sadie's mom, prop the front doors to the school open. Wind races in, rustling the papers on the check-in table and sending little droplets of rain in to sting our faces. I hold a hand up in front of my face, and then I spot a school bus parked in the circular drive out front.

I recognize Lance's dad and older brother helping people off the bus. Elderly people. My heart jumps. This is the bus from Sandpiper Active Senior Living! Which means that Bubby's here. As volunteers guide the seniors in toward the check-in table, I stand on my tiptoes to look for Bubby.

Old Mrs. Crenshaw, who was the town librarian forever and ever until Miss Suzie took over, is the last one off. The driver pulls the door closed and the bus lurches forward. I squeeze past my friends to reach Lance's dad.

"Mr. Travis, is there another bus from Sandpiper Active Senior Living coming?" I ask him.

He shakes his head. "They got all the residents onto this one, and the staff is coming over in their own vehicles."

"Are you sure?"

"Pretty positive. How come?"

"My bubby should've been on that bus." My heart is pumping into overdrive as I realize what's going on. Bubby's not here.

She's missing.

It's been two hours since the bus from Sandpiper Active Senior Living rolled in, and Bubby's still not here. No one knows where she is. I've sent her texts, Mom and Dad have called her, and nothing. No answer. We've asked every staff person who's come through the doors, and we get the same story.

"She left about noon with her scooter to go find Mr. Wheeler," they all say. "He'd gone out for a walk to the water to see the waves and was supposed to have been back. She refused to leave without him, and we're not a nursing home, so we couldn't force her to stay."

Dad alerted Officer Davis, who radioed Officer Rodriguez. He was going to search for them after he finished checking on Miss Worthington and Ike. Dad keeps pacing the lobby and threatening to look for them himself, but Mom's insisting he stay here. "Putting yourself in danger won't do anyone any good," she says. "Officer Rodriguez will find them."

Meanwhile the wind's been picking up, the rain is coming down even harder, and the meteorologists on TV are saying the storm might reach speeds of a hundred miles an hour, which would turn the hurricane into a Category 2. But they aren't sure if it'll come right at us or veer out toward sea. I don't care—I want Bubby here, right now.

"She's going to be fine," Sadie says for the millionth time. "I just know it."

"It's Bubby," Vi says. "She can do anything."

"I think it's sorta romantic that she took off to save Mr. Wheeler," Becca says with dreamy eyes. "Can't you just see them, clinging to each other in the wind, holding on together to fight the pushes of nature?"

"Forces of nature," I say in a monotone. "And no, it's not romantic at all. It's stupid. It was stupid for Mr. Wheeler to go down to the beach, and stupid for Bubby to go after him by herself, without a car. What if she doesn't come back?" My voice is rising as panic fills my chest.

"She's going to be fine," Sadie says again as she squeezes my hand. "She has to be."

But she still isn't here. Even an hour later, almost four o'clock, five hours away from landfall, she's not here. Officer Rodriguez radioed in to say that he drove all along Coastline Drive, stopping now and then to check the beach, and didn't see them. He's going to keep searching as he looks in on a couple more holdouts on the island.

The lights flicker as the wind gusts outside. Becca lets out a little shriek, and Vi grabs my arm.

"That's it, I'm going out to look for them." Dad shrugs on a Windbreaker as my mom tries to convince him not to go.

"Oh my God, y'all, I feel like I'm going to be sick." My stomach's churning all that lunch lasagna.

Sadie moves in front of me, a hand on each shoulder. "Lauren, it's going to be okay. I'm sure they just realized how crazy this storm is going to be, and they've gone into a store or something."

"But all the stores are closed and boarded up!" I know she's trying to help, but all I can think about is Bubby struggling to maneuver Wanda through the streets as wind and rain try their best to knock her down. "What if she's hurt?"

Dad's got his car keys in hand, and Mom finally lets go of him. Now Zach's trying to convince Dad to let him come too, and Mom's shaking her head.

The lights flicker again, and the front door flies open in the wind. Officer Davis and Mr. Alberhasky race forward to pull it shut.

"What is that?" Vi's dad says over the howl of the wind.

"I think it's a person," Officer Davis says, squinting through the sheets of rain.

"Bubby," I whisper. I pull away from my friends and run to the open door.

"Lauren! Get back here!" Mom yells.

But I don't listen. Instead I run until I'm just outside the door, standing next to Mr. Alberhasky and Officer Davis. The driving rain soaks through my long-sleeved shirt and jeans in seconds as I hold a hand up to my eyes to peer down the school drive. Sure enough, there's someone coming up the pavement.

Rolling, it looks like, not walking.

Bubby.

"Bubby!" I yell. I take off down the driveway, with all the adults on my heels.

She's riding Wanda up the driveway, but there's something weird about her. As I get closer, I see what it is—a man, perched on her lap. It's Mr. Wheeler.

"Hey, LoLo! Look what the cat dragged in!" she shouts through the wind.

She stops Wanda when I reach her, and Mr. Wheeler hops off. She stands up and I grab her in the squishiest, wettest hug ever.

"I was so worried," I say. "Dad was going out to look for you."

"Pish-posh. You don't have to worry about me," she says. "I'm tough old Bubby from the block."

I squeeze her even harder. Dad reaches us and throws his arms around us both.

"Let's get inside," he says. He keeps an arm around Bubby while I hold her other hand. No way am I letting her go now. Mr. Alberhasky fires up Wanda and rolls it behind us as Officer Davis helps Mr. Wheeler inside.

Bubby and I start shivering the second we step in the doors. Becca's mom throws blankets around both of us, and Mrs. Marks shows up with hot tea. My hair is plastered to my head—I hate getting my hair wet— and my clothes feel like they're glued to my body. But I don't care. Because Bubby's here and safe. Everyone I love is okay. Mom, Dad, Zach, Bubby. Josh is safe at school in Raleigh. My friends and their families are all here.

I reluctantly let go of Bubby so that we can get changed into dry clothes. A woman from Sandpiper Active Living hands Bubby her suitcase. In the bathroom, I pull on a pair of jeans. I yank my science flash cards out of the pocket of my wet pair. They're unreadable, the ink smeared and the paper tearing. I'll have to make new ones.

"Nothing like a dry pair of duds to make a woman feel like new," Bubby says as we stand in front of the sinks and try to do something with our hair.

I finally give up on mine and start laying out the flash cards that are still salvageable. I line them up on the little shelves that jut out from under the mirrors.

Bubby peers over my shoulder. "Were you studying?"

I nod. "I have to. I need to fix my grades. I can't let anything get in the way of that, not even a hurricane."

Bubby sighs and looks at herself in the mirror. "I sure do wish I had my blond wig," she says as she smooths her wet hair. "I hate for Mr. Wheeler to see me like this."

I smile at her. "You saved Mr. Wheeler's life. I doubt he'll care what your hair looks like."

"True dat," she says, and I cringe a little. "You know, this little rescue mission has reminded me that maybe there's more to catching a gentleman's eye than good looks. Like saving his behind from a hurricane."

My hair is starting to seriously frizz, so I pull a rubber band from my bag and try to collect it into a ponytail. "So, does this mean you won't be sharing flirting tips with Becca anymore?"

Bubby laughs, and my heart melts to hear it.

"Oh no, of course I'll still be doing that. Becca needs some of my sage advice on catching a young man's attention, after all." She gives me a side eye. "And you, too, my LoLo."

"No, thank you," I tell her. "The only thing I'm worried about is my grades. And RSVP. That's it. No boys."

Bubby sighs. "Extremes are dangerous, Lo Baby. And you miss out on so much. Trust me, I learned the hard way. Remember when dear old Mr. Vernon moved to Scotland this summer, and I didn't get so much as a kiss?"

I can see my cheeks tinging red in the mirror. Really, grandmothers should not mention kissing. Ever.

"That's because," Bubby goes on, "I was too focused on getting his attention. And the same with Mr. Wheeler. Until today, anyway." She shoots me a sneaky smile in the mirrors. "Think about it," she says as she scoops up her wet clothes and disappears out the door.

The lights flicker again. I should get out of here. The bathroom is the last place I want to be if the power goes out. Who knows what kind of creepy ghosts might haunt a middle-school bathroom. But I stay a minute longer, looking at my reflection in the mirror, bordered by those flash cards on the shelf.

Extremes, Bubby said. Am I being too extreme? I jumped from super-studious Lauren to good-times Lauren and then back to even-more-focused Lauren. Is there a middle ground? Somewhere that I can get As in school, do my extracurriculars, enjoy RSVP, and still have fun with my friends? Maybe even play a video game or two with Zach on occasion?

I feel like it's something that can't be planned, though. Something I can't jot down in my calendar for six p.m. to seven p.m. on Wednesday nights. Maybe it's just knowing when I've studied enough, or keeping my extracurriculars to a few really important ones. Maybe it's saying yes to an impromptu Saturday afternoon trip to the mall in Wilmington with Becca after finishing my homework, or combing the cove for shells with Sadie before jumping into RSVP business. Or maybe it's just more time spent in the *PPE* with my favorite friends, or lingering over dinner with my family once in a while.

If I let myself slow down, I feel like maybe—just maybe—I can find this balanced Lauren. The Lauren who knows how to have fun, still does well in school, and doesn't let herself get so caught up in the schedule of it all.

Then the lights flicker again, and I grab my bag and race out the door. I leave the flash cards on the shelves.

15

Becca

Daily Love Horoscope for Scorpio:
Something's brewing on the horizon. The winds will blow in with a big change, so brace yourself, Scorpio!

I mean, I for sure know that hurricanes are nothing to mess around with and I don't want any*one* or any*thing* to get hurt, but if I'm being totally and brutally honest, I completely l-o-v-e all the excitement in the air.

Drama is so totally my jam.

Besides, now that Bubby is safe and everyone else in town seems to be here (except for Alexandra, since Officer Rodriguez told us she and Ike refused to leave their house), it's cozy and warm and there's lots of laughter from little pockets of the room where groups of old dudes are gathered to play cards and little kids in pj's are listening to our town librarian Miss Suzie do a story time. If not for Linney trying to organize cheerleading practice in the center of the room, all would be perfect. Ugh. Like a giant swirling hurricane is going to be influenced by her cheer:

Blow your mighty, blow your best, blow right out of town.

'Cause we are fighting, we won't rest, and you can't keep us down.

It's been dark all day because of the storm clouds, but now it's getting to be night, and if I were home, Daddy would just be setting up the timer for my homework. (Let's just say I have a teensy-tiny problem sitting still and Daddy thought a butt-in-seat timer would keep me in place. FWIW: it doesn't.)

But no one (except Lauren) seems to care one itsy-bitsy iota about homework tonight. Plus, unless the storm blows out to sea, we're probably not even having school on Monday. We'd have to have morning assembly on cots in the middle of Mrs. Bishop's meditation shrine and the model-ships-in-bottles collection Mr. Hallowell insisted counted among the "essential items only" we were instructed to bring.

I rifle through my rolling suitcase for some appropriate shelter wear. What does one wear to a hurricane evacuation? I packed tons of options, naturally (I can do "essential items only" as well as the next person), but from the looks of it, the proper attire seems to be either sweats or pajamas. And I don't do sweats.

Pajamas it is.

I find my cutest matching flannel set—navy with hot pink, light pink, and white polka dots—and slip off to the girls' room to change. I grab my sparkly toiletries bag while I'm at it, so I can brush my teeth. And then I add my strawberry lip gloss, because hello, this may be a giant sleepover, but there are *boys* around.

And not just boys, but Philippe. I wonder what he thinks of all this. Do they even have hurricanes in France? Maybe I should go ask him. I may possibly have casually noted him setting up a cot near Lance and a couple other guys from the soccer team earlier (and by "casually noted," I mean I could tell you he sleeps on a blue ticking-striped pillow, brought a DS with three games in the case, snacks on ruffled potato chips, and knows how to make a bed with hospital corners—you know, casually noted). Maybe I *should* go ask him.

Except I've kind of been avoiding him ever since

B-Day (Braces Day). I doubt he'd be interested in talking to a brace-face anyway. I sigh and survey the room instead. Mama and Daddy are over by the back doors talking to Mayor Keach. Vi is helping her dad set up a folding table by the stage for a couple of giant coffee urns, and Lauren is against the wall, actually doing her homework, although she said she'd be up for hanging out as soon as she finishes all her math problems. Weirdo. I hunt for Sadie and finally find her in a big circle with Izzy and a bunch of girls who look like they're around the same age as Iz.

I plop down in the middle of them. "What's happening, *chicas*?"

The girl on the other side of Sadie sniffles, and Sadie removes her arm from Izzy's shoulder and turns to the girl. "We're just missing some furry friends over here," Sadie says.

The girl has big brown eyes, and they're all watery when she looks at me.

Awww. Poor thing.

"I want my puppy," she says.

I share a look with Sadie, who says, "Her parents took her dog to the animal shelter in Wilmington so he'd be safe during the storm."

"Oh," I say. "Well, hey, tell you what. Do you know Cooper at Polka Dot Books?"

The little girl nods.

"Well, he's my next-door neighbor, and he's basically the best dog there is. And *he's* at the same shelter. So I'm betting he's taking really good care of . . ."

I pause and wait for her to fill in her puppy's name.

"Oscar the Grouch," she offers. I raise one eyebrow and avoid Sadie's eyes so I don't laugh.

"Right. Oscar the Grouch. I bet little Grouchy is having the absolute best time of his life with all those other doggies to play with."

She nods and gives me a big smile, and I look around at the other girls. They're only a couple of years younger than we are, but they look so small and lost. Was I ever that little? Yipes.

"That doesn't seem that fair, though, does it?" I ask. "How come they get to have all the fun and we don't? I think we need to do something about it. I say we have a . . ." I motion to Sadie to yell at the same time as me, but she just looks at me with big question marks in her eyes, so I have to yell, "DANCE PARTY!" solo.

All the girls squeal and jump up. I find my phone and plug it into my glittery portable speaker (obvs I packed the true essentials) and crank up a happy tune. A few adults look over with pursed lips, but then they go back to their boring talking and we girls boogie down. I even get Lauren to ditch the homework once she spots us. When she decides to excel at something, she's all Lauren about it, and ever since the Scottish party this summer, where Lauren totes let loose on the dance floor and started having Fun with a capital *F*, dancing is her thing. I love it.

I'm midspin when I happen (just *happen*, I swear) to glance at the soccer boys, and I almost fall over when I catch Philippe watching me. Watching ME! Omigosh, I seriously could die right on the spot. I don't even know what to do, besides clamp my lips closed over my braces, of course. I duck my head and do another shimmy-thing move, and when I peek back at him, he's facing Lance. Bummer. But he *was* watching me, and I saw it with my own two eyes. *Oooh la la!*

After the girls are all worn out from the dance party, Sades and I help them find their parents and then Sades goes to tuck Izzy in since her mom has joined Vi's dad in handing out coffee to the grown-ups. I consider trying to sneak a cup myself in case Philippe happens to glance over again, so I can look all grown-up and mature, but

I'd feel pretty guilty about using up the shelter's entire supply of cream and sugar.

Instead I wait for Sadie and then we wave over Lauren and Vi.

"You guys want to go peek out some windows?" The gym at our school is in the middle of the building—on purpose since most schools around here have to double as storm shelters—and doesn't have any windows that could blow in during a storm. But that also means we can't tell what's happening outside here.

"Are we allowed to leave this room? Since everyone's here and the cafeteria's closed now?" Lauren asks, glancing around.

"I mean, the bathrooms are in the hall, and we've been going there all night," Vi says.

"Duh. Right."

We head in the direction of the bathrooms but then peel off down the hallway that leads to the main office and the doors outside. When we reach them, we each push one of the four heavy side-by-side doors open halfway and peer outside. It was eerily calm when we drove over to the school late this morning, and even though you could kind of smell the storm in the air and the clouds looked pretty creepy, you couldn't really tell anything big was coming. But obviously it was way worse by the time Bubby showed up, and now the winds have picked up even more. The trees are bending over, and in front of the school a plastic cup bounces across the sidewalk before getting lifted off the ground and disappearing high into the sky. It's super weird to think that on the other side of the bridge Sandpiper Beach is basically a ghost town. I cross my fingers on both hands and make a wish that we get to go back home to everything looking exactly the same.

"Okay, that's long enough!" Lauren declares, pulling on my pajama shirt to yank me back inside. "We came, we saw. Now let's get back!"

Sadie and Vi clang their doors shut too and we all turn. The hallway is in nighttime mode, with only about a quarter of the overhead lights on, and the wind rattles the heavy doors. Something slaps against the outside of one of them. None of us want to admit we're scared, but we all jump a little at that.

"Let's go," Sadie whispers.

"Cosigned," I say.

In the distance, from the direction of the cafeteria, a lone figure walks slowly toward us. Uh-oh. Are we about to get in trouble for wandering the school without a hall pass? Or worse? We all stand frozen as the shape draws closer.

Wait.

Is that . . . ?

Yippity skippity! It's Philippe!

My hand automatically flies to my mouth to cover the Metals of Evil. When he reaches us, he looks kind of shy, and his eyes bounce all around but don't really settle on any of us.

"Um, *bonsoir*," he says, kind of in my direction, but he could also be talking to Lauren. It's hard to tell.

Sadie answers. "Hey! Coming to check out the storm?"

"Er, yes. I mean, *non*. I was . . ." He trails off and then takes a super-duper deep breath and looks STRAIGHT at me. "Do you feel like talking?"

Do I feel like talking? Do *I* feel like talking? Do seagulls poop on Sadie's head? Well, maybe that was just the once, but yes. Yes, they do. Of COURSE I feel like talking with Philippe!

"Sure," I answer breezily. I can do breezy! Except, well, my voice might have cracked a little, but whatevs. Otherwise? Totally breezy.

Sadie and Lauren giggle, and even Vi looks a little wide-eyed as she says, "Um, okay, so we're gonna go

234

pull our cots together and get settled in. Just, um, come find us when you're done talking, Becs."

"Yup." That's all I can manage. Philippe has his hands stuffed in his pockets, which looks like a super-good plan because I have zip-zero idea what to do with my own hands. Flannel polka-dot pajamas are seriously lacking in the pocket department. I stand there shuffling awkwardly while my three friends abandon me. Well, maybe not abandon so much, because it's not like I don't want to hang out alone with Philippe, but . . .

What could he want?

"Would you care to . . . I mean, do you wanna zit?" The word "wanna" sounds weird in his French accent, like he's just trying out American slang. And don't get me started on "zit" versus "sit." Of course I don't want a zit. Who would? I hold in my giggle, though, and when he motions to a spot in a little alcove between the trophy cases, I slide down the wall. He sits next to me and crosses his legs in front of him.

"So, uh, I wanted to say zat it was really nice what you did wiz zose leetle girls earlier. Helping zem not be scared, Becca."

I pretty much love the way my name sounds when he says it. "You saw that?"

"You know I deed because you saw me watching you dance."

"Oh." BUSTED! "Um, right. I didn't . . . I didn't know you knew why we were dancing, though." Smooth, Becs. Really smooth.

"I did. I noticed. I always notice you, Becca."

My heart is *thunk-thunk*ing in my chest because he's sitting so close to me, but when he says that, it, like, totally stops. For a second I think I might actually need those paddle thingies they have on TV hospital shows to restart it, and I get a little panicky. But then it hammers against my ribs, and I let out my breath with a whoosh.

He always notices me?

I've always wanted to be always noticed by someone!

"You . . . you do?"

"Oui." I can feel his nod. I can't see his nod because I'm too afraid to look at him, but when I screw up my courage, he's looking right back at me, and his eyes are soft and have this kind of hazy expression. Oh. Oooooooh!

Philippe likes me. Like, LIKE likes me! Whoa.

I look back at him, and I'm betting my eyeballs are big and wide because I'm kind of registering all of this, and then they get even wider because he moves his head a tiny bit closer to me, and if he does that even one more time we will totally TOTALLY be kissing, and I think maybe I want him to move one more time but at the same instant I think maybe my heart will stop again if he moves one more time, and omigosh I think he *is* moving one more time, and is this the part where I'm supposed to close my eyes or do I wait until his lips actually touch mine and thank the goddess I put on my strawberry lip gloss and . . .

And then it goes dark.

Not eyes-softly-closed-because-I'm-being-kissed-for-the-very-first-time dark. Nope. It goes pitch-black-dead-of-night-because-a-hurricane-just-knocked-out-the-power dark. I guess I must have been leaning forward, because I bump into his chest. His arms come around me and hug me. Whoa again.

Some red emergency lighting comes on overhead, and I wait until my eyes adjust some before leaning back a little to look up at Philippe. His arms stay around me, though, and it would be *très* romantic if we weren't in the middle of, y'know, a hurricane. Whatever. It's still *très* romantic.

"I really like you, Becca. You are so sweet and nice to everyone, and you make Sandpiper Beach feel a leetle more like home for me," Philippe whispers into the darkness.

"I do? But I've barely talked to you. And I have braces!" Ack! Why did I say that? Awkward alert!

Philippe laughs. "So what? Every time I see you, you are so happy and bubbly and you always have a smile for me. Well, until you got braces, zat eez. Can I tell you a secret?"

I nod. But then I don't know if he can see that, so I clear my throat and say, "Yes." It comes out sounding all hoarse and weird.

"I zink braces are cute. On you, at least."

I snort before I realize that is sooo not ladylike or romantic. Whoops. "Oh, puh-leaze. They are not cute. And they still hurt a tiny bit. Well, not much. But some-times. And there are all these foods I can't eat and they don't match any of my outfits and no one will ever want to kiss me now and—"

Oh. My. Gosh.

I did NOT just mention kissing in front of Philippe. I did not. Except I totally did. I would definitely be okay with Principal Carney showing up right now and giving me detention for life for being in the hallway outside her office. Technically, I'm not in her office or even doing anything wrong, but I wouldn't even plead my case. Nope. Not one bit.

"*I* would want to kiss you," Philippe says. "I mean, I *do* want to kiss you." He is studying the floor to avoid looking at me when he says it, but his fingers find mine and lace through them. His palm is warm. It feels right.

"You ... you do?" I ask. I think I might more squeak it than ask it.

Philippe nods. I don't know what to say, so I just squeeze his fingers. I guess this is the right thing to do, because he turns to look at me again, and by now my eyes have adjusted enough that I can see his. (It helps that our faces are *thisclose*.)

"Um, okay," I say.

And then he does. He tilts his head a little, and somehow I just know that I'm supposed to do the same thing in the opposite direction, and then his lips are on mine and I barely have time to register before it's all over and I just HAD MY FIRST KISS.

And it was perfect!!!!

Now what? Are we supposed to do it again?

"Becca?" A beam of flashlight sweeps down the hall, and Vi's voice calls my name. Philippe scrambles to his feet, then holds out his hand for me again and pulls me up. He squeezes my fingers softly once more before Vi reaches us. Right away her flashlight aims at our hands, and I can hear the smile in her voice when she asks, "Are you okay? We didn't know if the lights in the hallway were connected to the generator."

"Oh, um, they're not," I answer.

Vi laughs out loud at that. "Well, yeah. Since I'm standing in the hallway now, I can see that!"

"Right." I'm so totally flustered and I kind of want to be all alone to process my first kiss but I also kind of want to be alone with my best friend so I can tell her all about it and then I also *also* kind of want to be alone with Philippe so maybe he will kiss me again. And possibly I want to do a happy dance or possibly I want to collapse on my bed—I mean, cot—and fall into a deep sleep because this kissing stuff is *beaucoup* confusing and does this mean Philippe is my boyfriend now or what?

"The generator didn't come on right away," Vi says. "My dad had to go out and fix it. Like, out in the storm. It was kind of amazing, actually." She smiles for a second, like she's imagining Mr. Husky as the Superhero of the Hurricane. Which he prob is. "But it's running now. And the radio is hooked up to the generator too, and there was just a report that the storm is weakening and turning a little. People are saying the worst is gonna miss us!"

Philippe squeezes my fingers again, and I turn to face him. He's staring at me with this big goofy grin on his face, and it makes my insides go all melted buttery.

Oh.

This is gonna be just fine.

Everything is gonna be just fine.

Vi

16

SIMPLE CINNAMON ROLLS

Ingredients:

1 cup nondairy, unsweetened milk (e.g., almond milk)

½ cup butter, divided

1 packet of instant yeast

¼ tsp salt

¼ cup and 1 tbsp sugar, divided

3 cups all purpose flour

¾ tbsp cinnamon

canola oil (to coat mixing bowl)

1 can of cream-cheese frosting

Pour the milk and 3 tbsp of butter into a microwave-safe bowl and heat in the microwave in 30-second increments until the butter is warm and melted (not boiling). Let it cool a little before you sprinkle on the yeast. Let this sit for 10 minutes (to activate the yeast), and then add 1 tbsp of sugar and the ¼ tsp of salt. Stir the mixture. Add in ½ cup of flour at a time, while stirring. When the dough is sticky and becomes too thick to stir, take it from the bowl and put it on a lightly floured surface. Knead the dough for a minute or two and form it into a loose ball. Rinse the mixing bowl, coat it with canola oil, and put the dough back in. Cover the bowl with plastic wrap and set it on the countertop to rise for about 1 hour. The dough will double in size. Next, on a lightly floured surface roll the dough out into a thin rectangle. Melt 3 tbsp of butter in the microwave and brush the melted butter onto the dough. Top it with ¼ cup of sugar and ¾ tbsp of cinnamon. Roll the dough tightly, starting at one end. Then turn it so the "seam" is facing down. Cut the roll into sections that are about 1½ to 2 inches wide (a knife works, but you might find that dental floss works better!). Put the rolls into a buttered 8" x 8" square pan or an 8" round pan. Melt the remaining butter and brush it onto the tops of the rolls. Cover with plastic wrap and set on top of the oven (to rise again), and preheat the oven to 350°. When the oven is preheated, bake the rolls for 25–30 minutes (or until golden brown). After the rolls cool, you can frost them with cream-cheese frosting.

**SO yummy!!!
**Lots of fun to make at a sleepover. You can make them the night before and then eat them all up for breakfast in the morning!

*P*sst, kiddo. Wake up." Dad's voice rumbles softly into my dream about playing soccer in a huge hurricane. I've just kicked the ball, but the storm has picked it up and is pulling it higher and higher into the sky. Linney's on the sidelines cheering for the hurricane while Lance laughs his head off.

Basically, not such a great dream.

So I crack an eye open to see Dad squatting alongside my cot. He's already dressed in old jeans and a flannel shirt, Tar Heels cap squarely in place. Exact same thing he wore yesterday. I blink and sit up. "Did you go to sleep at all?"

He shakes his head. "Needed to make sure that generator kept going all night. Couldn't leave all these folks in the dark."

I look around the gym, which is dim in the emergency lighting. Almost everyone is still asleep. I cover a yawn that can't help escaping. "What time is it?"

VI

"Early. About five. Sorry I woke you up, but I need your help."

I nod and reach over to pull on a sweatshirt. If Dad's been up all night, the least I can do is get up a little early to help him out. I slip on my shoes quietly so I don't wake up my friends. Lauren's buried under her covers, Becca's snuggled up with her old stuffed dog, Mr. Bobo, and Sadie is frowning in her sleep, probably working out how we're going to deal with Miss Worthington.

"That's my girl," he says, beaming. He leads the way through the maze of cots and snoring people. Honestly, it's weird having a giant sleepover with everyone in town. Even though I've done this a few times before, I learn something new every time. Like, I never knew that Mrs. O'Malley slept in dog-printed pajamas and that Mrs. Travis used a sleep-apnea machine. We scoot around Lance and a bunch of guys from soccer, zonked out near the front of the room. That's pretty weird too.

I follow Dad out the gym door and down to the cafeteria. Then we go back behind where we all line up for lunch on normal days, to the kitchen area. Now, this is extra strange, because I never in a million years thought I'd be in the school-cafeteria kitchen. I bet the secrets of that weird "meat loaf" they serve every other week are buried back here somewhere.

We pass a few other adults cutting up food and cracking eggs into giant bowls, and then Dad stops in front of a big coffee machine. "I know you can make a killer pot of coffee at home. Think you can do it for a thousand people?"

"Sure." I mean, there's not much to making coffee. Just adding the right amount of grounds and water.

Dad shows me the huge carafes that'll transport the coffee from the cafeteria back to the gym—the same ones we set up yesterday. So, basically, I have to make about a hundred pots of coffee. Or something. Dad moves to take a look at one of the ovens that Ms. Sanders, our next-door neighbor, insists isn't heating up fast enough when I have the best idea.

"Hey, Dad? While the coffee's brewing, can I make a bunch of cinnamon rolls for everyone?"

He smiles. "You bet, sunshine. I think people would love that." And then he's across the room, tool belt on, listening to Ms. Sanders go on and on about how she needs the oven to heat faster than it is.

I've got about ten pots of coffee done and have rolled out dough for a few batches of cinnamon rolls when

Ms. Sanders says—really loudly—"I knew you could fix it! Thanks, David!" She throws her arms around Dad in a hug, everyone else starts clapping, and his face flushes redder than I ever thought possible. I get it, though. All this attention is So Not Dad.

"Well, um, glad it's fixed," he finally says.

Mr. Gilbert slaps him on the back. "Hiring you was probably the best money the school board ever spent," he says. "Between the generator yesterday and this oven, and the way you've kept the school up this fall. We all thought the board was going to have to shell out for a new scoreboard in the gym, until you came along and got it working again."

Dad goes even more red, and my heart swells just a little, seeing everyone appreciate his hard work.

"I love the work, and helping the kids," he finally manages to say. "So . . . well, if we're all set, then, Vi? Let's get that coffee moving." Dad backs toward me. I'm pretty sure he just wants to get out of the spotlight.

"These are full." I gesture at two of the big carafes.

"If I carry them, can you open the doors?" he asks as he hefts the enormous jugs of coffee off the floor and into his arms. They're so big, he can barely even see over the tops of them.

I quickly start yet another pot of coffee and drape some plastic wrap over the batches of half-made cinnamon rolls to let them rise, and then I dart ahead of him to hold the kitchen door.

When we get to the gym, Dad carries the coffee to the same tables it was set up on yesterday. A few people spot it and actually clap. I guess near-miss hurricanes call for coffee first thing in the morning.

Dad goes beet red again as he sets the carafes down on the table. Immediately, people swarm the cups still sitting out from yesterday and go to fill them with piping-hot coffee. Dad steps back next to me, and together we watch the first few people sample their cups. No one makes a face, so I guess I didn't mess up too badly.

"You did good, Vi," Dad says to me, arm around my shoulder.

"So did you." I grin up at him. "I have to finish those cinnamon rolls, though."

"Then let's get at it. I need to go survey the damage outside."

Back in the kitchen, I make more and more pots of coffee and, with help from Ms. Sanders and Mrs. Fenimore (how weird is it to bake with your science teacher?), enough cinnamon rolls to feed the crowd in the gym. I put the last batch into the (now functioning) oven just as the first hungry townspeople make their way into the cafeteria. Dad comes back in from outside and talks to Mr. Travis and some of the other adults while I grab us both plates of food. We eat a quick breakfast standing in a corner of the kitchen.

Dad checks the time on his phone. "I need to go and help clean up out front so people can get their cars out. It could've been a lot worse, but the wind knocked down a big tree across the driveway, and there's a lot of debris all over."

"I'll help you." All of this helping is kind of nice. I like it.

Dad smiles at me, and I like that, too.

"David?" Mr. Travis sticks his head into the kitchen. "We're headed out now."

"Be right there," Dad says.

I stuff the last of my eggs into my mouth and snag the rest of my cinnamon roll to eat on the way. We drop our plates onto the dishwashing stack and leave the kitchen. I wave to a bleary-eyed Becca, standing in line for food with her parents. I'm pretty sure they made her get up early to go be useful too. Becca doesn't intentionally see any daylight before ten o'clock on the weekends.

After I change (quietly grabbing clothes so I don't wake up Sadie and Lauren), I go outside to join Dad. The wind and rain have stopped, but it's still pretty overcast. And there are branches and leaves and small tree limbs everywhere. Someone's lined up a row of huge trash cans, and a few people are gathering the debris and dropping it in.

I find Dad down at the bottom of the circular drive, near the road. He's surveying a big tree that's fallen across the driveway with Mr. Travis, Lance, Lance's older brother Sam, Coach Robbins, and Ms. Purvis.

"We can use my truck," Ms. Purvis is saying. She's wearing an old SOMETHING'S FISHY IN SANDPIPER BEACH fish-cannery jacket and torn jeans and basically doesn't look anything like Ms. Purvis, seventh-grade homeroom and history teacher.

"All right. I'll get the chain saw," Dad says. "We'll have this thing out of here in no time."

Ms. Purvis backs up her old truck and pops the tailgate, just in time for Dad to get back with the school's chain saw. Lance and I heft up pieces of big limbs and toss them into the truck bed while Mr. Travis and Ms. Purvis handle the trunk. I'm kind of thankful that the chain saw is really loud. That keeps me from having to try to talk with Lance. I haven't had anything to say to him since he turned into Linney's little lapdog.

In no time at all the tree is off the driveway and filling up Ms. Purvis's truck. It's cool outside, but we're all drenched in sweat. Dad pulls off his cap and swipes his forehead with the back of his hand.

"What next?" Mr. Travis asks.

Dad scopes out the school grounds. More people have come out and are spread across the driveway, lawn, and parking lot, picking up debris and putting it into trash cans they've dragged outside.

"Looks like we're in good shape out here," Dad says. "Folks can start leaving, if everything's clear on the roads and the island. I'll stay behind and clean up the school."

"Not alone," Ms. Purvis says, as she climbs into the driver's seat of her truck. "I'll round up some more people to help out as soon as I get this out of the way."

As Dad, Lance, Sam, Mr. Travis, and I walk back up toward school, Dad talks to everyone we meet on the way. A "thanks for helping!" here and a "great work!" there. Everyone smiles at him, and most of them thank him too.

Something creeps into my heart. Something different. I think it's pride. . . . I'm proud of my dad, the school janitor.

Just inside the doors, Mrs. Marks and some other people are gathering the check-in lists and folding up the tables. Becca's wheeling a giant trash can full of coffee cups through the lobby. She's glaring at it and is barely touching it with two fingers. I'm like 99 percent sure that her dad insisted she help out. I'm just dying to know how she got stuck on trash duty instead of entertaining the little kids or handing out coffee creamers.

Dad stops to help Mrs. Marks fold up the sticky leg of one of the tables. Linney's standing nearby—not helping, of course, just sipping her coffee (or *milkfee*, as Becca likes to call it, based on Linney's milk-to-coffee ratio) and holding up the wall. Her highlighted hair looks a little bedraggled in its low ponytail.

A crash sounds from across the lobby, and I think we all jump a mile. Becca lets out a horrified wail as she surveys the plastic trash can, tipped over onto its side, cups and empty sugar packets still tumbling out all over the floor. She looks like she's about to cry. She bends down to pick up the cups. I take one step toward her to help when Linney detaches herself from the wall and sashays across the trash-strewn floor.

"Don't worry about that, Becs," she says, like she and Becca are besties. "The *janitor* is here. He'll clean it up. It's his job, after all." She sips daintily from her milkfee and eyes me over the top of her cup.

I glance back to where Dad's still helping Linney's mom. If he heard Linney, he's not saying anything. Instead he's pounding at the table leg, which refuses to budge. But plenty of other people heard. Lance is right next to me, frowning at Linney. A few other kids from school are standing around, holding sleeping bags and backpacks. And Lauren and Sadie have just wandered into the lobby, still in their pajamas.

"*What* is taking him so long? Seriously, you'd think this school could hire someone who'd actually do his job. I mean, just last week I found a hair in one of the bathroom sinks. Gross." She shudders, as if this is the most disgusting thing in the history of the world.

That's it. I clench my fists and stride forward.

"You have a lot of nerve," I say to Linney.

Her smile falls just a little bit. I don't think she expected me to say anything. Which just makes me want to say more.

She pastes the smug smile back on. "Please, Violet. Your dad is kind of useless when it comes to cleaning."

And that does it.

"My dad is *amazing* at his job. In fact, he's pretty amazing at everything. Like setting up all the cots before anyone else got here yesterday, and organizing the check-in so the police would know who was still on the island. Saving the whole town from staying overnight in a dark school. Rescuing breakfast this morning. Cleaning up out front so everyone can leave today. And he's even helping your mom right now. So what are *you* doing, huh?" My voice is way too loud, but I don't care.

What I do care about is the look on Linney's face, which is half shock and half embarrassment. I'm just about to add, "Don't let your tongue get your teeth knocked out," but I bite my own tongue.

"I think you've said enough, Linney," Lance says quietly from next to me.

"Now make like a cheerleader and hop," Becca adds, her arms crossed.

I don't have the heart to tell her that doesn't make any sense at all. Not when she, Lauren, and Sadie are all lined up like soldiers, ready to pelt Linney with empty coffee cups if she says anything else. And Lance . . . I can't think about that right now.

Linney rolls her eyes, lets out a sigh louder than anything, and stomps past her mom and right out the door. As I watch her go, my heart starting to slow back to normal, I catch Dad's eye.

He's smiling. And blinking kind of fast. He takes off his cap and swipes at his face, like he's trying to wipe off sweat. But I think—no, I'm pretty sure— those are almost tears. I want to race to him and give him the biggest hug he's ever had, because, really, he is the best dad ever. Janitor or not. He kept us all safe during the storm last night. But I don't right now, not in front of all these people. Instead I grin at him. He winks at me and goes back to helping Mrs. Marks. He knocks that table leg into place with one good *thump*.

"Now, that's the Vi I know," Lance says from behind me.

I'd almost forgotten he was there. "Um, thanks," I say. Because I'm really not sure what to say to that. But when I catch his eye, he looks at the floor.

"You know, Linney and I were never . . . um . . . and at the dance, I didn't really want to . . . you know . . ."

He trails off and finally meets my eyes. "She's not very nice, is she?"

"That's pretty clear, Captain Obvious," I say, and it feels almost like we used to be. So I smile, not even one tiny bit mad at him anymore. What he just said to her a few minutes ago told me everything I needed to know.

"See you at soccer. Maybe you can come by the restaurant after. Free tater tots for friends of the owners. Unless they run away. No tots for runaways." He slaps my back, and I could swear his hand stays on my shoulder just a little longer than it needs to.

And it doesn't feel weird at all. It's kind of nice, actually.

Mrs. Genevieve Worthington

together with

Mr. and Mrs. Lawrence J. Malix

invite you to share their joy

at the wedding of their children

Alexandra Elise Worthington and *Isaac Jacob Malix*

on ~~Saturday November 14~~ Sunday November 15

at two o'clock in the afternoon

at the

~~Church of the Victorious and Forgiving Holy Redeemer~~

~~1401 Live Oak Drive, Sandpiper Beach, North Carolina~~
banks of the Bodington River, end of
Bodington Drive, Sandpiper Beach, North Carolina

Reception to follow at

~~Poinsettia Plantation House~~

~~10370 Poinsettia Road (on the mainland)~~
the same place!

The favor of a reply is requested by October 25

Dress: Elegant Vintage

17

Sadie

TODAY'S TO-DO LIST:
☐ there is not enough paper in the world
to make this list, so let's just leave it at
THROW WEDDING!

*N*OW should I worry?"

My mom glances over at me as we drive back home from the shelter, er, school. She looks all Zen because our house will still be standing when we get there and not riding a wave somewhere out in the Atlantic. "What's this now?" she asks.

"Well, all yesterday morning and at the shelter you told me to concentrate on packing and boarding up the house and not to worry about the wedding until we knew there was something to worry about. So I just want to know when I'm supposed to start worrying that there's supposed to be a giant ceremony tonight when, um, our entire town looks like the Big Bad Wolf huffed and puffed all over it."

Mom bites on her bottom lip as we swerve to avoid a fallen tree branch in the road. Up ahead a power line dangles loosely from its pole, and the sidewalk is basically a solid carpet of sticky wet leaves.

"I'd say commence the freak-out," Izzy chimes in from the backseat.

"Not helpful, Iz," my mother replies. "Sweetie, let's just take things one at a time. When we get home, we'll call Alexandra. Cell service is out, but the landline should work. We'll see where her head is. For all we know, she'll want to postpone. Maybe riding out that storm scared her into being a rational person. And *if* she wants this wedding to go forward as planned tonight, we'll just take a deep breath and improvise."

I steal a glance at Mom. "We?" I murmur.

"Yup. *We.* I'd be honored to be your assistant. If you'll have me, that is."

Assistant? All this time I've been hoping that Mom would hire me back to her company (even if I might not accept because of RSVP, it would still mean the world to be asked) and now *she* wants to work for *me?* For a second it feels like I've landed in Oz, but it was a hurricane that (almost) hit yesterday, not a tornado.

"Me too! I can help!" Izzy says. "I can do the photography, like at the *Little Mermaid* wedding!"

I turn in my seat to give her a grin. "That would be great, Iz. Thanks."

Mom catches my eye as I turn back, and her own eyes are soft. "The Pleffer girls ride again, huh?"

I love the sound of that. I really, really love the sound of that. All of a sudden, even though I know this could be asking for major headaches, I kind of sort of hope that Alexandra Worthington insists the wedding go on as planned.

"Sadie-babe. Tonight's wedding is off! O-f-f. Off."

I twirl the phone cord around my hand in the darkened kitchen. Darkened at ten in the morning because the power is out at our house and everywhere else in Sandpiper Beach. "Oh, but . . . I thought . . . um, is everything okay with you and Ike?"

"With me and Ike? Of course. Why would you ask that?"

"Oh, because when you said the wedding was off, I—"

"No, no. The wedding is on. Ike is my forever guy. I said the wedding *tonight* is off. You should see the utility pole that crashed through our roof. Sadie-babe, I tell you: the wind. And then the noise. And the hole in the roof. It rained on my shoe closet. Thank goodness I wasn't at that silly shelter and I could rescue my Manolos."

"Your—?" I don't have a clue what a Manolo is, but I guess I never will because Alexandra doesn't let me finish. As usual.

"I made Ike sign a contract stating we can get off this godforsaken island just as soon as we say our 'I dos.' Why you people would want to live here under the constant threat of hurricanes is beyond me."

Maybe because we're not under *constant* threat and because most sane people leave the island and seek shelter when there *is* a threat and because there are about six zillion amazing things about Sandpiper Beach that make the very occasional risk of a hurricane totally worth it. But I know better than to argue with Alexandra Worthington.

Instead I say, "Um, so about those 'I dos.' When do you think—"

"Tomorrow. Two p.m. sounds right. We have to deal with all the pesky insurance people today about our roof, and Ike is very insistent that we have to be here to meet with them. Hmph. But tomorrow afternoon I want to be at the altar saying my vows, and furthermore, I want this to be the best wedding anyone has ever seen. No exceptions. Now, I want updates every hour."

Of course she does.

When I hang up, I find Mom prying one of the plywood boards off the window outside our living room. "We have twenty-eight hours!"

Mom drops the board. "Wtty httt hnns?"

I cock my head and crinkle my forehead. Mom removes the two nails she had pulled out of the window and was "storing" between her teeth. "I said, 'Twenty-eight hours?'"

"Yep. And I quote: '*furthermore*, I want this to be the best wedding anyone has ever seen. No exceptions.'"

Mom just laughs. "Of course she does. Well, let's get to work. I have a feeling, if nothing else, it's going to be the most unique wedding anyone's ever seen. Especially with the electricity out all over town and half the roads blocked by downed branches. I'd say, first things first, you need to organize an RSVP meeting ASAP."

With cell-phone towers out of whack because of the storm, I have to call Becca, Lauren, and Vi on the regular phone instead of issuing the Bat Signal by text as usual, but forty minutes later we're all in place at the *Purple People Eater*. Even Mom and Izzy.

"Does this bottled water taste off to anyone else, or is it that it's so warm?" Mom asks. Lauren looks like she's about to seriously lose it, while the rest of us just giggle.

"It's just warm," Becca, Vi, and I all say at once. I hand Mom a flashlight from the bucket.

"It's cozy down here," Mom says, switching it on. Izzy just sighs happily. She's been angling to get in here since preschool, practically.

We all turn to Mom to get us started, but she glances right back at us with her eyebrows up. "Don't look at me, ladies. I'm just the hired help! This is your show."

Becca shoots me a smile. "Totes. We got this, girls."

Except we have major obstacles. For one thing, Mom, Izzy and I went back to the mainland to check on the Poinsettia Plantation House before coming to the marina and discovered bad wind damage to their wraparound porch. The only person we could find working was a maintenance guy who said they would be closed for at least a week. So much for a reception site.

The Church of the Victorious and Forgiving Holy

Redeemer had some flooding from all the rain. No ceremony site.

In trips back and forth from the *PPE* to the marina's office phone, we find out that the caterer evacuated to her sister's in New York City and won't be back in time, the florist's supplier is farther up the coast where the storm made landfall and all his greenhouses are in disarray, and the minister who was supposed to perform the ceremony fell off a ladder when he was boarding up his house and is in the hospital with a broken leg. To sum it up, that means we have:

1) no venue for either the ceremony or the reception,

2) no food,

3) no flowers, and

4) no one to do the actual marrying

But aside from that, everything will be amazing.

As if.

"Girls, could I make a suggestion here? I don't want to tell you how to run your business, but I do just want to point out one thing I've learned over the years."

Mom waits until we're all looking at her and says dramatically, "We live in the best town on earth."

We all stare, while Mom waits patiently. When Becca says, "Ummm . . . ," Mom sighs and adds, "What

I'm saying is that the greatest part about living in a small town is that everyone knows everyone else. Okay, fine, so maybe that's also sometimes the worst part. But at times like this, trust me, you'll be glad. I'm going to leave you all to ponder that while I go chat with your mom, Lauren."

When Mom leaves, we continue to stare blankly, trying to figure out the message she was giving us.

Finally Izzy says, "Do you think she means we should just ask everyone to pitch in?"

Lauren nods thoughtfully. Then she pulls out her lucky test-taking pen from her bag. "I think that might be exactly what she meant. Sades, get your notebook out. We've got lists to make."

The power is still out the next day, with only hours to go before Alexandra Worthington's wedding. No, scratch that. The electricity is out, but we have plenty of power.

Manpower, I mean. (And womanpower!)

"Sadie, where do you want these?"

I glance up at Principal Carney, who's holding two hanging baskets she's taken the flowers out of and filled with bottles of sunscreen and bug spray. "I thought we could string those from the branches over there so guests can spot them as they head to their seats," I say, pointing at the tree I have in mind.

"Oh, yes, seats. I've got two from my dining room. I would have brought more, but my car is so tiny, even those were a tight squeeze," Principal Carney says.

I smile and point at the clearing of grass along the banks of the marshy Bodington River, where at least three dozen mismatched chairs are lined up in neat rows with an aisle down the center, awaiting the ceremony. "That's okay. You'd be surprised how fast a couple from here and a couple from there add up." The assortment is mismatched, but the overall effect fits perfectly with our vintage wedding theme.

"Oh, lovely. Everyone really chipped in. And blankets? Where do those go?"

"See Lauren for that one. She'll be here in a few, and then she'll be setting them up on the other bank, where there's a bigger grassy section. The tide's on its way out, so you can wade across easily if you go that direction," I say, pointing again.

When we realized none of the places in town could accommodate a large wedding on zero notice, we came up with the idea of having it outside. The beach was too windy and noisy with the surf still rough from the storm, but the tidal river is sheltered and quiet and peaceful. Exactly right for a wedding. Luckily, the warm weather came back, and it's a perfect fall day.

I sigh happily as I look around. Over by the ceremony site, Lance is setting the Victorian fans I made last month on chairs. Becca and Philippe are hanging lace curtains donated by Becca's mom from a low tree branch on a live oak at the top of the makeshift aisle. Alexandra Worthington can come through them to make an entrance when the ceremony starts.

Mom and Izzy are stringing the lace doily–wrapped mason jars from other tree branches around the clearing along with these cool lace balls the three of us made last night by papier-mâché-ing more doilies to balloons and then popping the balloons inside once they had dried. They're so pretty and mystical-looking.

I wander to the spot we've designated as a parking lot. Vi and her dad are staking a sign they created by nailing strips of wood one on top of another and painting one word on each. It reads HAPPILY EVER AFTER STARTS HERE, and the last branch has a painted arrow showing the way to the ceremony site.

"You guys, that's so cool and romantic! I love it!"

Vi and her dad share a grin. "We're pretty proud of it," Mr. Alberhasky says.

I'm just happy to see Vi and her dad smiling at each other. It seems like they've totally worked out all the janitor stuff now.

I consult my clipboard and ask Vi, "Hey, have you seen Lauren yet? We need to get going on the reception setup."

Before she can answer, a loud clanging noise makes all three of us turn around to face the parking area. Lauren rides up in her golf cart, which has approximately forty-seven tin cans tied to the back of it, dragging along the dirt path and making a racket that's sending birds into the air. When she gets closer, she spins the cart around so we can see the giant JUST MARRIED sign pinned to the back. "Like the getaway car for the bride and groom?" she yells. "Mom and Dad let me drive again after I told them it was an emergency. And everyone at the marina pitched in to decorate it!"

"Everyone pitched in" is kind of the motto for this wedding. We spent a big part of yesterday going door-to-door, and not one single person turned down our requests for help, even if they were doing their own storm cleanup. By late afternoon we had the site all cleared of downed branches, tons of offers of food for the reception (it definitely helped that people were already cooking the remains of their freezers before all the food spoiled in the power outage), and Mrs. Mize, the high school algebra teacher, and Mr. Rose, the Sunday school teacher from the Church of the Victorians and Forgiving Holy Redeemer, lined up to play music for the ceremony.

We also had an offer from the kazoo band that marches in the Fourth of July parade, but I didn't think Alexandra Worthington would be up for that.

Despite her insisting on updates every hour, cellphone reception is still so bad because of the storm damage that the only time we've talked has been when I've been at home to take a call. Meaning not a lot. She's going to be in for a huge surprise today. On the one hand, it's not exactly (read: at all) what we planned these last few months, and Alexandra Worthington isn't really a "go with the flow" kind of person. But she wanted a Sandpiper Beach wedding, and there's nothing more Sandpiper Beach than this wedding! If she doesn't like it, it will only prove she isn't human. I'm hoping for the best, since it's all I can do.

Our last stop yesterday was Sandpiper Active Senior Living. We still needed someone who could do the actual marrying part, and we'd heard there was a retired minister living there. Bubby met us at the door.

"What's this I hear about a wedding?"

Lauren filled her in as quickly as she could.

"Well, you've come to the right place, that's for sure," Bubby said. "I'd be honored, obvs."

I looked at Lauren, but she just stared right back at me blankly. Finally Becca said, "Honored to help us find Mr. Biggs? Um, okay. If that's the word you want to go with."

"Find Mr. Biggs? Pshaw. We don't need him. You have Bubby!"

Lauren's eyebrows went sky high. "Um, *have* Bubby? What does that mean."

"Lo, honey. You remember Old Lady Edna? She used to forget her teeth on a regular basis and it totally grossed you out?"

Lauren nodded slowly, and Bubby went right on talking. "Well, last year she up and married that handsome fellow Stanley. It was a giant scandal on account of how much younger he was. Everyone thought he was a gold-digger, but I knew true love when I saw it."

Becca breathed, "True love. *Très* romantic. But how young *was* Stanley?"

"Barely seventy-five. Gotta give Old Lady Edna credit—teeth or no, she could reel in the gentlemen, that one. Anyway, no one else supported their marriage, but I was all for it. That's why they asked me to officiate the ceremony."

"You? Bubby, you married them?" Vi asked.

"Sure did. Got ordained on the interweb and bada bing bada bang, I was in business. Certificate's still valid. Now, what time do you need me there?"

And really, how do you say no to Bubby?

Speaking of Bubby . . . "Is our minister all in place?" I ask Lauren now, gesturing upriver.

Lauren rolls her eyes, but smiles. "Yep. She's all nestled into Vi's kayak at the curve in the river. Shuffleboard Dan is going to give it a shove into the water when the time comes, and then she'll paddle up at the perfect moment. It's not quite Elvis, like Alexandra Worthington requested, but she *is* wearing a hot pink muumuu and sequined Chucks—and waiting on your mom's signal."

This is definitely going to be a wedding to remember. Exactly like Alexandra Worthington wants.

"Sadie, where do you want this?" I spin to see Dr. Bernstein and Officer Davis struggling with a giant mirror framed in gold leaf.

"I was hoping we could prop it near the food tables over by the reception site. Dr. B., can you write out the menu selections on it using these markers?"

I hand him special markers that write on glass and will erase when we're done.

"Sadie, I'm a doctor. You know the reputation we have for our handwriting, right?"

"Oh please, Dr. B. You're a *dentist*."

He sighs deeply as I tuck the markers into the pocket of his jacket. "It'll get done."

"Thanks!" I call after him and Officer Davis as they wrestle the mirror up the hill. Becca and Philippe pass them on their way down, holding hands. It's so weird to see that, but I have to admit, they look really good together. And happy.

"How goes it, peeps?" Becca asks.

I consult my clipboard again. "Decorations are pretty set. We still need to spread out all the blankets we collected to make them look like mini picnic spots. Each one gets a pillow and a teacup candle in the center, only we won't be lighting them when the sun goes down because of all the flammable fabric. Just for decoration. Then someone needs to organize all the food that people dropped by and—"

Becca cuts me off to say, "Mrs. Marks and Lance's mom are already doing that. Mrs. Travis brought a bunch of food from Stewie's, too, so it's almost like this thing will be catered. But better!"

"I hope they left out the liver and onions. Eww. But awesome otherwise," I say. "I think we're mostly set. Becs, do you have the bouquet for the bride?"

"Yup! It's in my bike basket, hang on!"

When we found out we couldn't get flowers for the wedding in time, we thought about going around town and scrounging for them in gardens, but not that many flowers are still blooming this late in the year, and we were already asking everyone for so much else, and we didn't want to clean out their yards, too. Then Becca had the brilliant idea to take all the costume-jewelry brooches from the collection she'd begun at the Founder's Day yard sale to make the bouquet. Since then she's bought about a gazillion more off eBay (when the girl commits to a collection she commits), and Bubby contributed a ton of her own brooches to the cause.

Becca used a piece of colored card stock to make a paper cone and nestled a Styrofoam ball inside it like it was a scoop of ice cream. Then she took all the jeweled pins and poked them into the Styrofoam until every last inch was covered. With a long trailing ribbon tied to the cone, it's the most beautiful bouquet I've ever seen. I *hope* Alexandra will agree.

I trail Becca to the makeshift parking lot. "I expect guests will start arriving any second. We've got people stationed at just about every corner in town to direct any out-of-town cars this way."

I smile at that image. I've loved Sandpiper Beach my whole entire life, but never more so than right this very second.

"I think we're ready," I say, crossing my fingers and hoping for the best.

18

Lauren

exhilaration noun \ ig͵zilə'rāsh(ə)n \
a feeling of happiness or excitement
Use in a sentence:
Sadie, Becca, Vi, and I are full of exhilaration that
we've pulled this wedding together at the last
minute. And that we never, ever, ever have to see
Alexandra Worthington again.

*A*nd here comes trouble," Vi murmurs when Mr.
Elldridge's black SUV swoops into the last bit of street
parking we had saved for the bride.

We all take one huge, collective breath and step
toward the car. Once everything got set up, the four of
us ran over to the marina and changed—although we
agreed to ditch the nice shoes for sturdy boots instead.
The riverbanks are still a little muddy from the storm.

Mr. Elldridge beams at us as he walks around to open the back door for Miss Worthington.

"Wait a moment," she snaps just as he cracks the door. "I'm still fixing my eyelashes."

Hands up, Mr. Elldridge backs away from his car.

"It's all right, Daddy," Becca whispers to him. "We'll take it from here. Thanks for being the chauffeur."

"Anything for my little girl," he says. "Good luck."

I could swear that he speed-walks away to the river site where everyone's waiting.

"I think you'll be happy with what we've pulled together," Sadie says, in an only slightly trembling voice. "It looks really nice."

The window slowly slides down to reveal Miss Worthington, decked out in her wedding dress, her hair up and with a (huge) sparkly tiara perched on her head. "Sadie-babe, what about the glider?" she demands, waving a mascara wand for emphasis. "I already had to do my own makeup. The least I can get is the glider. Is it coming?"

"Well," Sadie says, "the runway at the little airport over in Live Oak Beach wasn't clear of debris yet, so—"

"What you're saying is that I don't have my glider."

"Right . . ." Sadie trails off.

I try to pick up where she left off. "But you should see what you *do* have. It's pretty amazing."

"What about my éclairs? You, Red, did you find my éclairs?"

Becca's eyebrows shoot up into her hair. "We were in a *hurricane shelter*," she says.

"And?"

Sadie sighs. "We couldn't get any éclairs made in time, but we do have last-minute catering—sort of— and I promise it's some of the best food you'll ever taste."

Miss Worthington makes a *hmph* sound. Somehow I don't think she's going to dig the barbeque from Stewie's or the Variety Shoppe's famous boiled peanuts. She doesn't say anything as she swipes at her eyelashes. When she finishes, she doesn't get out of the car.

That's not good.

I look to Sadie, who's deep in thought. Finally, she blows her bangs out of her eyes and reaches up to start to pull her hair into a ponytail before she remembers that her hair's been "done" by Becca, who'll lose it if Sadie messes it up.

"Look," she says. "You just need to come out and see it. Everyone pitched in, and it's going to be a wedding to remember."

Miss Worthington gives Sadie a withering stare. Then she surveys the rest of us. "Why is Blondie still blond?"

Vi opens her mouth, probably to tell Miss Worthington exactly where to stuff it, but before she can say anything, Miss Worthington starts talking again.

"Is the string ensemble here?"

"No—" Sadie says.

"What about my out-of-town guests?"

"Well, a little more than half of them are here. The ones who got in before the storm hit or who drove in today," Sadie answers.

"Half?"

"More than half," Sadie says in a small voice.

I'd have thought that one was pretty obvious. A hurricane usually means no one is flying in or out of town. She should be thrilled that a bunch of them did get here. But I know by now that logic isn't Miss Worthington's strong suit. Not by a mile.

Miss Worthington is actually glaring at us now. "I don't understand. I *hired* you to create my perfect day, and yet—"

Just then Ms. Mize, the algebra teacher/musician, swoops in and inserts herself between us and Miss Worthington.

"I know we haven't met," she says in this bubbly voice, "but I have to tell you how wonderful it was to see most of the town out helping people find their way to this wedding! And only most because I think the rest are here doing other stuff. It's just all so charming and quaint. Everyone must think so much of you."

"Ms. Mize plays the violin and agreed to step in when the string ensemble couldn't make it down from Wilmington," Sadie explains.

Miss Worthington just blinks at Ms. Mize, who smiles at her and then excuses herself to get into place for the wedding march.

"I'm . . . confused," Miss Worthington says.

"The guides," I fill in. "We asked people who weren't coming to the wedding to help direct the traffic here, so that both the out-of-town guests and Ike's local guests could find the new venue."

"Oh, I . . ." Miss Worthington touches her makeup case, and I'm pretty sure she was too busy looking at her face the whole ride over to notice any of the guides.

"And this is for you." Becca unwraps the brooch bouquet from its pink tissue paper and holds it out for Miss Worthington.

She stares at it for a moment. Then she slowly opens the door and emerges from the car, white lace wedding dress cascading around her and the white sparkly tennis shoes Sadie convinced her to wear when the wedding relocated. She takes the bouquet and holds it as if it's something breakable.

"I hope you like it," Becca says.

Miss Worthington just nods, still looking at all the little brooches that make up the bouquet.

"Do you think she likes it?" I whisper to Sadie.

Sadie shrugs. It's hard to tell with Miss Worthington, especially when she's oddly silent like she is now. It makes me think of how the others told me she acted at the cake tasting.

"Well, let's, um, head this way." Sadie points toward the riverbank.

As Miss Worthington takes a few steps forward, Becca eyes the train of her dress dragging across the damp ground with this horrified look. She tosses the tissue paper from the bouquet to Vi, and gathers up the material to keep it from getting dirty.

Miss Worthington stops abruptly in front of the sign that Vi and Mr. Alberhasky made. Becca stumbles a little, and I reach out to catch her arm. Miss Worthington points at the sign. "What's this?" she asks in a sort of wobbly voice.

I peek around her. Oh my God. Miss Worthington is actually getting teary! I sort of expect a comet to hurl itself across the sky, or the tides to reverse completely.

"Dad and I made it," Vi says. "Do you like it?"

"Do I like it?" she repeats, sounding a little flustered. Her little smile pretty much answers Vi's question.

"Everyone pitched in," Sadie says.

I point across the grass, where a group of people are milling around—not guests for the wedding, but people we all know and see every day. "Principal Carney brought a mirror from home that we could write the menu on for the reception, and Miss Suzie, the librarian, collected quilts and blankets to use for seating. Mrs. O'Malley gave us a bunch of lace doilies she made, to use for decorations."

Everyone in the group, dressed in jeans and sweatshirts, is smiling at Miss Worthington. A few people wave, and Jonathan, Principal Carney's four-year-old son, shouts, "You look so pretty, Miss Westy-ton."

"I don't understand. I'm just . . . I can't believe you got so many people to help. How did you convince them all? They don't even know me." Miss Worthington pats at her eyes, probably trying to banish those tears I saw before they ruin her makeup.

"Well," Sadie says. "Even though you're new here, you're one of us now."

"This is the kind of thing we do in Sandpiper Beach for one of our own," Becca adds.

"But how?" Miss Worthington asks.

"We put out the call, and people came. Got it all done in two shakes of a sheep's tail," Vi says.

"Just like that," Miss Worthington murmurs. "You ladies have outdone yourselves. This entire town has outdone itself." And then she strides off toward the group, bouquet in hand, and Becca racing to keep up without dropping the train.

When the rest of us catch up, Miss Worthington is moving down the row of townspeople, shaking their hands and telling each one of them thank you. Even cute little Jonathan, who hugs her around the leg. "I want all of you to come to the wedding," she says.

"But none of us are dressed up," Miss Suzie says.

Miss Worthington waves her bouquet. "Who cares? I just want you all to be there."

"Hmph!"

I turn around to see where that grumpy noise

came from. An older woman in a cloche hat and stuffy-looking vintage dress stands behind us. One of Miss Worthington's out-of-town guests, I guess.

She turns to the man on her arm and says, "I had to go to every vintage shop in Cincinnati before I found this hat! And now she's letting *anyone* in!"

The woman stalks off toward the riverbank, and Miss Worthington actually giggles. Giggles! Like a happy kid instead of a stressed-out, bossy adult.

I poke Sadie with my elbow, and she smiles back. This may be going even better than we'd hoped.

"Now where's my Ikey? I want to get married!" Miss Worthington says. And with that we lead the way toward the river.

We stop behind the lace curtains that hang from tree branches. I peek around them and spot Sadie's mom up near the front, coordinating with the musicians, so we hang back with Miss Worthington as she waits to walk down the "aisle" (which is really just a carpet of flower petals from the end-of-season mums at the town florist's).

"I'm sorry I got a little . . . over-the-top with the wedding details," Miss Worthington says out of nowhere.

None of us know what to say.

"I got so fixated on making everything perfect and unique that I forgot the entire point of the wedding," she goes on.

"Love," Becca fills in.

"Exactly." Miss Worthington gives her a smile. "You all look very nice, by the way. And thank you for everything you've done."

"You're welcome," Sadie replies. I think her shoulders actually sag just a little in relief, like she's just put down the weight of carrying around this wedding.

"Oh, no!" Miss Worthington's eyes get huge. "I completely forgot my something old, something new, something borrowed, something blue!"

Becca grins. "Oh, we can totes fix that! Can't we, girls?"

"You bet," I say as I fish in my tiny, impractical purse for the shell I found washed up at the marina this afternoon when I went to pick up the golf cart. "Here." I hold it out to Miss Worthington. "This is a Scotch bonnet. It's the official state shell. It can be your something old."

Miss Worthington holds up the little brown-and-white shell, admires it, and then says, "Thank you, Lauren."

She slips the shell into one of her white gloves, where it looks lumpy, but she doesn't seem to care.

Sadie pulls the red ponytail holder from around her wrist and winds it around the "stem" of Miss Worthington's bouquet. "This is your something new. And it's red, which is good luck in weddings in India."

"And your something borrowed." Becca slips a black button into Miss Worthington's glove, where it clinks against the shell. "It's one of Mr. Bobo's button eyes," she explains. "It fell off at the shelter, and I didn't want to lose it."

We all look to Vi. "Something blue," she says. "Um . . . well, all I have is this." She pulls a little compact out of one of her dress pockets and flips it open. It's dark blue eye shadow—which exactly matches what she's wearing on her eyes. I guess we've all gotten so used to seeing Vi wearing makeup and dresses now that none of us even noticed.

"You have *eye shadow* in your pocket?!" Becca's equal parts surprised and proud.

"Yeah. Don't make a big deal about it, okay?" Vi swipes a little color on the brush. "I promise just to put a tiny bit on so it doesn't ruin what you already have," she says to Miss Worthington.

And—surprise to end all surprises—Miss Worthington closes her eyes and lets Vi apply just a teeny bit of the navy blue to her eyelids.

"Are you nervous?" Vi asks Miss Worthington as she slips the compact back into her pocket. All eyes are on us as we wait behind the lace curtains (which, truthfully, don't really hide us), and I'm sure Vi is remembering how it felt to walk the runway at Linney's birthday party last summer.

"Not at all," Miss Worthington says. "I'm marrying the love of my life. I have nothing to be nervous about." And with that she gives Ike, who's standing near the riverbank, a little finger wave. The old Miss Worthington probably would've freaked out if her groom had seen her in her dress before the ceremony started.

Becca sighs, all smiley and dreamy-looking.

The musicians—Ms. Mize with her violin, Mr. Rose with his banjo, and (thankfully) no kazoos—start playing. Bubby rows up in her kayak (I may very well have the only grandmother on the island who can kayak) and steps out with help from Sadie's mom. She's dressed in a blinding pink muumuu with Hawaiian flowers all over it. And peeking out from under the hem are the sequined Chucks that I caved and got her for her birthday earlier this year. Not my best moment, but Bubby sure was happy.

Sadie's mom signals to us.

And the wedding starts. Miss Worthington floats down the aisle toward her Ike. Sadie, Vi, Becca, and I slip into chairs in the back. Izzy flies around, snapping pictures and probably reveling in her role as official wedding photographer.

"Do you, Alex—you don't mind if I call you Alex—take Ike to be your lawfully wedded hubby?" Bubby asks Miss Worthington.

Vi snorts when Bubby calls Miss Worthington Alex. But Miss Worthington doesn't even seem to notice.

"I do," she says, all dreamy-eyed. "But only if he agrees that we can stay here, in that lovely house by the ocean, close to all these lovely people. Would that be okay, babes?"

Ike's face goes from surprised to confused to thrilled in all of five seconds. Then he says, "Of course that's okay!"

Bubby beams at them. "Do you promise to honor, cherish, and save him from hurricanes?" she asks. "Like I did with my Mr. Wheeler—hi there, cutie patootie!" She winks at him in the audience. "He was near certain death by the sea when I rolled up and scooped him onto my Wanda, and drove off with him into the sunset."

"More like into the howling wind and driving rain," I whisper to Sadie.

"I do" is all Alexandra says.

"And do you, Ike—you're a cute one, aren't you?—take Alex to be your lawfully wedded wife?"

Poor Ike actually blushes. "I do," he finally manages to say.

"Do you promise to honor, cherish, and always do what Alex says?"

We all have to cover our mouths to keep from laughing when she says that. But Ike says, "I do."

When Bubby says, "You may smooch the bride," I'm pretty sure I could dive under the chair from embarrassment, but the whole crowd laughs, and Alexandra and Ike kiss.

It's all pretty perfect, actually.

After the ceremony, everyone moves to the reception area, which is really just a bunch of blankets set up picnic-style with pillows. Lance and his family make sure the food from Stewie's and the dishes everyone brought are ready to go, and Vi floats over to help him.

Ms. Mize and Mr. Rose put aside the sedate wedding

music and break out some serious down-home fiddle-and-banjo tunes. Everyone's eating and dancing and talking and having a great time. Even Alexandra and Ike are whirling around the "dance floor" like crazy, Izzy buzzing around and taking about a million pictures of them.

I'm dancing in a tiny circle with Becca and Sadie, all of us beyond excited about how well this whole thing has gone, when Bubby swings by on Wanda with Zach. I'm wondering exactly how she managed to talk my brother into dancing with her. "Fab wedding, ladies," she shouts to us. "I'm booking you in advance for mine." She gives us a wink. "That ain't a two-step, Zach. It's more like a twenty-step. I need to give you some dancing lessons," she scolds my brother as they shuffle away.

"I don't think we'll have to worry about Bubby getting married here," I say to Becca and Sadie. "She'll just skip off to Vegas."

Vi and Lance are out on the dance floor too. When Ms. Mize and Mr. Rose switch from a really raucous tune to a slow ballad, Sadie and I take that as a signal to check on things, leaving Becca to find Philippe. It looks like Vi and Lance are going to try the slow-dance thing all over again—and this time Linney's nowhere in sight.

In fact, I haven't seen her at all since the shelter yesterday morning. She's probably at home, fuming over how Vi finally told her off.

Sadie and I check on the food, arrange the gifts that are piled on the little red wagons that people brought to use as gift tables, and make sure the cake is ready to go. Just as we finish making the rounds, the ballad ends and Vi and Lance and Becca and Philippe join us.

Lance and Philippe discuss the finer points of European soccer teams (while Vi jumps in now and then with opinions).

"What are we going to do, now that we'll have all this time that isn't taken up by wedding planning?" Vi asks.

"Study," I answer. "Obviously."

"Plan more parties," Sadie says.

"Or another wedding!" Becca says. "Bubby was totally hinting earlier."

"No. No way." I fix Becca with my best glare. "Vegas, remember?"

"Can you believe we actually pulled this off?" Becca asks. "I mean, with all the crazy stuff that's happened? Not just Bridezilla and the hurricane, but with Linney being jerktastic to Vi the whole time."

"And us pretty much stealing this wedding from Sadie's mom," Vi says.

"Lauren and me getting booked for the Great Headlight Incident," Sadie adds.

"We didn't get booked," I remind her. "But I did get that awful grade."

"Even more tragic than that," Becca says, "my braces."

"Most tragic," Sadie says, trying not to laugh.

"Worse than the hurricane, for sure," I add.

"The only thing more horrible than Becca getting braces would be like the entire island falling into the ocean," Vi says.

We laugh so hard that we have to grab each other to keep from collapsing.

"Whatever!" Becca says. "Just wait till y'all join me here in Metal-land. Then *I'll* be the one laughing."

And that just makes us laugh harder. Lance and Philippe take a few steps away, as if we'll infect them with our craziness.

"Seriously, though," Becca goes on. "The thing is that when I think back on it all, none of that stuff was really *that* bad. Even the hurricane. Or at least it wasn't as bad as it would have been if I didn't have you guys around. It's weird, but even the worst stuff is better when we're together. Is that totally cheesy? Because if not, I may have to write a song about this phenomenon."

Vi nods. Sadie rubs her eyes. And I grab everyone into a huge hug.

"What are they doing?" Lance whispers to Philippe.

"I don't know, but eet looks scary," Philippe replies.

"Let's go get some more boiled peanuts."

Philippe makes a face, but disappears with Lance.

"Okay, way too much seriousness," Becca says. "And now that the boys are gone, let's talk about my kiss some more!"

When the sun goes down, the entire riverbank is lit up with white battery-operated strings of twinkle lights and these amazing glowing glass jars that Vi and Mr. Alberhasky made using the stuff from glow sticks. The music's still going, full speed, and the guests are dancing. Alexandra and Ike have been smiling the entire time. The whole scene gives me this warm, melty feeling.

After slurping down Drumsticks and ice-cream sandwiches from Lily Lemon's ice-cream truck, which has pulled up right in the middle of the road to serve ice cream to all the guests, we snag a couple of the Polaroid cameras lying on the picnic blankets. Instead of having a traditional guest book, Sadie came up with this great idea to have all the guests snap pictures of themselves to paste in the book along with their messages.

"Stand still!" I yell to Vi, who's got Sadie balanced on her shoulders. They stop moving for a split second, and I take the picture right before they tumble to the ground.

"Selfie!" Becca shouts. She throws her arm around my shoulders and we grin into her camera.

Vi's waving her picture around like that'll make the image appear faster (it won't—the picture develops as a chemical reaction happens in the layers of the photograph under a compound of silver), and Becca's making a kissy face into the camera for Sadie, when Philippe joins us.

"Hello, *mes amies belles*," Philippe says in his accent. "May I tell you again that you look very neece tonight."

Becca grins and says, *"Mercias."* And she probably has no idea that she just mixed up the French and Spanish words for "thank you."

Philippe laughs. "Let me take a peecture of you all."

Becca tosses him her camera. We all wrap our arms around each other and flash huge smiles under the moon and the twinkly lights, music and laughter floating around us. There's no one else I'd rather be with tonight. Even after all the crazy stuff—my awful grade, the Great Headlight Incident—I'd do it all over again just to have this night with my best friends.

"Say cheez!" he says.

"I have a better idea," Vi says. "Ready, girls? One, two, three . . ."

"RSVP!"

ACKNOWLEDGMENTS

We have so many people to thank for getting this book into the world, but first—and most important—thank *you* for reading *You're Invited Too!* You're the reason we write books in the first place, and the fact that you chose this one to read means everything to us.

Our little book would not be what it is without all the enthusiasm and guidance from our editor at Aladdin, Amy Cloud. Amy, thank you for not asking if we'd lost it when we told you the girls were going to plan a wedding. They're totally ready to plan yours, too (Sadie's already got a list made). And if it gets too crazy, Bubby's standing by to bail you out. Thank you for loving these characters as much as we do. Another huge thanks to everyone at Aladdin—Teresa Ronquillo, who patiently puts up with all our marketing questions; Faye Bi, publicist extraordinaire; Marilena Perilli for such gorgeous covers; Laura Lyn DiSiena for the adorable interiors; and managing editor Katherine Devendorf.

A grateful thank-you to Jack and Ben Malone, who made sure we got all the soccer action right. It's weird to thank Pinterest, but seriously, thank you, Pinterest people, for pinning all those awesome wedding ideas. And, of course, we have to thank the communities of Ocean Park, Maine, and Oak Island and Southport, North Carolina, for letting us squish them all together and come up with Sandpiper Beach. A bear hug (or twenty) to the teachers and librarians who champion children's books and recognize their enormous power—you make us look good, and we wouldn't be able to do what we do without your support! A huge thanks to our comrades in pens (computers?), the MG Beta Readers, for endless cheerleading and writerly commiseration. Love you guys!

A few extra notes from Jen:
I'd like to thank my agent, Holly Root, for always having my back and being a voice of gentle wisdom in Crazy Publishing Land. To my (happily) ever-expanding writing community: it's such a privilege to share shelf space (and, in some instances, crepes) with you amazing people,

especially my friends in SCBWI-NE, in OneFourKidlit, in Binders, and at the Writer's Loft. My family gets lumped in here, but in truth, you guys are the best and biggest part of my life, and I have mad love for you all. But you know that.

And a little more from Gail:
A great big thank-you to my most fabulous agent, Julia A. Weber, for responding to all my crazypants, six-paragraph e-mails with simple, thoughtful responses that somehow magically make me step back, take a breath, and realize that everything really is going to be okay. Thank you for believing in everything I write. There is not enough cake in the world! Another thank-you to the ladies of Team Weber; the LL&N critique group; everyone in Midsouth SCBWI, Fearless Fifteeners, and Binders; my nonwriting friends who remind me there is a world outside of books; and everyone at St. John's. Most important, to my family and especially my daughter—I love you all! Thank you for your patience and unwavering support.